LIGHTNING MARY

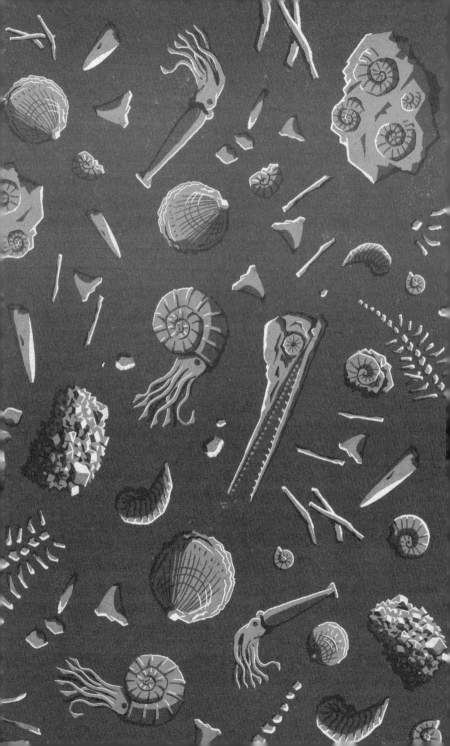

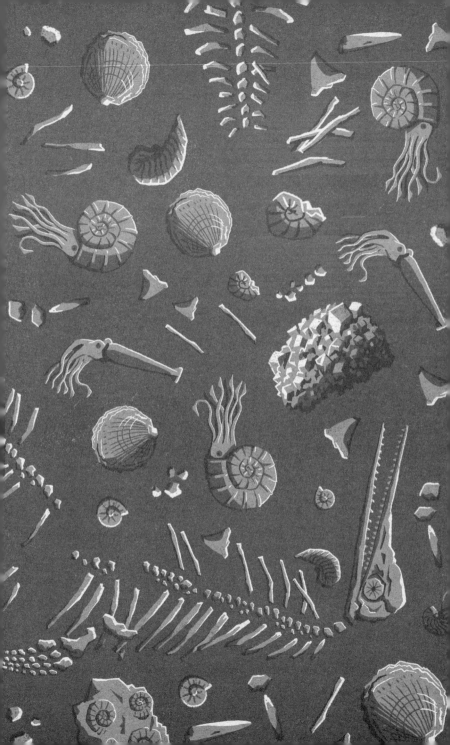

LIGHTNING MARY

ANTHEA SIMMONS

ANDERSEN PRESS

First published in 2019 by
Andersen Press Limited
20 Vauxhall Bridge Road
London SW1V 2SA
www.andersenpress.co.uk

2 4 6 8 10 9 7 5 3 1

British Library Cataloguing in Publication Data available.

ISBN 978 1 78344 829 6

This book is printed on FSC accredited
paper from responsible sources

Printed and bound in Great Britain by Clays Ltd, Elcograf S.p.A.

To my wonderful scientist son, Henry,
for his encouragement (nagging!) and his
pride in his old mum.

To all the readers out there. It's your talents
that matter, not the package they come in.
Mary did not get the recognition she deserved in
her lifetime because of poverty, gender and
class. Don't let anything stop you. Go for it!

PART
ONE

PROLOGUE

*T*isn't everybody gets struck by lightning and lives to tell the tale.

But I did. Not that I recall. I was only a baby. My father wasn't there when it happened but he would have told you the story if you'd asked him and would have recounted how he found me wrapped in a cloth, quite gone from my mind. Like dead. But not.

It was the night the circus came to Lyme Regis. Jugglers and fools. Bearded ladies. Performing monkeys. Dashing riders on powerful steeds, performing amazing acts, so folks said. More like showing off on a pony, if you ask me.

A neighbour of ours, Elizabeth Haskings, took me to see the spectacle, perhaps as a kindness to my mother who had just given birth to another stillborn, or so she could use me as a reason to get up close enough to see the riders' handsome faces.

There was an almighty storm. Rain lashing down like

something out of the Bible . . . Noah's flood, maybe. The lightning lit up the sky over and over again and the thunder was like ten thousand rocks bouncing down from the cliff face and into the sea. Elizabeth held me tight in her arms as we sheltered under a huge tree with two others. All screaming, no doubt. Except me. I am not, nor ever have been, a screamer.

A bolt of lightning struck that tree, a mighty elm, and split it in two. But it didn't stop there. It struck Elizabeth and the other folk and frizzled them up like fat in a pan. Elizabeth dropped me like a stone when it struck her.

My father heard word that I was dead with the rest of them and he threw his chisel aside and ran up from his workshop fast as he could, with terror in his heart and tears in his eyes. Some folk had carried me back home and put me in a basin of hot water to try to bring me back, but I reckon it was only when I heard my father calling: 'Mary! My Mary! Come back! Come back to me!' that I drew breath again. I think it would have broken his heart to lose two Marys.

It is strange that I should have so nearly been burned. There was another Mary before me. My big sister, she would have been. She burned away in a trice in a terrible fire. Mother never spoke of it, but I know what happened. Left for a moment in a room full of Father's wood shavings, she tipped over the lamp and *whoosh*, she was gone!

And then I came.

They do say I was a dull, sickly child before the Lord smote me with his lightning and that I burned brighter after; but I don't know about that. All I know is, something lit a fire in my being and it wasn't the lightning . . .

1
DEVIL'S TOENAILS
AND SNAKESTONES

I loved my father. He was the best father in the world. My mother was always too busy with the babies when I was growing up. She kept having more of them to replace the ones that died. I am the second Mary in this family, as I told you.

I never paid the babies much attention. They were always crying or screaming . . . or dying. Mostly dying. Then Mother would be wailing and refusing to eat. Father had a sad look about him for a day or two, but once they were in the ground, he'd be off to the cliffs, all alone at first but then, at long last, he started taking me and Joseph with him.

Joseph was born two years before me, but we were thick as thieves. We did almost everything together when we were small and I loved him nearly as much as I loved Father. Nearly.

Mother said it was a good thing that Joseph was so kind as to play with me because I didn't have many friends.

The girls and boys at Sunday School were silly creatures.

They didn't work hard. They just laughed and skipped and wasted time. I couldn't be doing with them. Once, one of the girls, Emmie, tried to tie up my hair in ribbons. She said I must try harder to be pretty or I would never have a husband. What a fool! I have never cared to be pretty. Better to be strong or clever, or strong *and* clever, and I didn't need a husband for that!

I was about six, I think, when Father first took me hunting for dragons' teeth and the like. Why would anyone choose to play with a doll or sing silly rhymes whilst jumping over a rope, when they could be finding treasure?

I had been wanting to go with Father ever since I could remember. The stories he told me when I was a little child! The treasures he brought back! Crocodile teeth, all white and sharp. Snakestones. Tiny serpents curled up in the rock, changed into stone by saints in days gone by and flung far out to sea. Father said if we got them wet they might wake up and wriggle away or bite us with their venomous fangs!

He let me hold them. I'd wrap my fingers round them as hard as I could in case they started squirming. Sometimes I thought I could feel them trying to squeeze through my fingers and escape but when I looked, there they were, imprisoned in their little rock.

Ladies' fingers were hard and shiny, not like ladies' fingers at all. Some folk call them thunderbolts but Father never did back then, maybe because he thought it would frighten me, reminding me of the lightning strike. But as I got older, he started calling me his little Lightning Mary when I was being clever, asking good questions about the treasures and such.

Then there were the Devil's toenails . . . Now, you'd think they'd be scarier than ladies' fingers, wouldn't you? But I never minded them. They do look like a great, big white toenail, though! Ugh! I should think the Devil would have black toenails. Or maybe red.

When I was very little, these treasures were like magic to me and I wanted to find some for myself more than anything in the world. Father said I was like a puppy, snapping at his heels, begging for attention. 'Persistent', he called me. I liked that. I like persistence, so long as I get whatever I am persisting for.

Anyways, one day – a Sunday it was – my father jumped up from the table and announced that he was taking me fossicking on Black Ven. Mother straight off began to scold him. She was always trying to stop his 'little expeditions' as she called them. Usually she was cross because she thought he should be working to put bread on the table.

But this time it was different. She did not want him taking me to Black Ven. Even I could tell from the name that it was a bad place. It doesn't sound like a good one, does it? Sounds like a place the Devil might hide, waiting for poor souls who stray from the path . . . especially on the Lord's Day when they should be in church or praying or, where I should have been, at Sunday School.

'It's a dangerous place, Richard! You can't take the child! Why, only a week last weren't there two killed in a landslip? Besides, don't you always say how important her learning be? Why take her away from school on the one day she can go?' she pleaded.

I ignored the bit about school. I would have been very sorry to miss it usually, but Mother's pleading had had quite the opposite effect. Two killed! I felt a shiver go down my spine but it wasn't fear, I can tell you. Plain excitement.

Mother must have seen the look on my face because she started arguing harder than ever.

But my father wasn't having any of it. He'd made up his mind to go, and go he would and take me with him, whatever she might say. She tried hiding my boots but Joseph found them and helped me put them on my feet before she could utter another word.

'You coming too?' I asked Joseph as he stood up and brushed the dust from his knees.

He winked at me. 'Not I! Ezra, Nathan and I are off up the field to fly Ezra's new kite. You can have Father to yourself for once!'

I felt another shiver of excitement. I pulled my bonnet on

and wound a comforter around my neck, for it was a bitter winter's day.

Father pinched my cheeks. 'We'll get a bit of colour in that pale little face of yours and more learning than in a whole week of school!' he said.

'If you don't get her killed first,' muttered Mother under her breath. 'Seems like I am the only one God-fearing enough in this heathen household and tis left to me to pray for your souls.'

Father snorted and then tried to sneak a kiss from her but she shrugged him off. He chuckled. He knows her ways.

'There'll be time enough for prayers when we get home again, Molly. The good Lord don't begrudge a man time spent teaching a child to marvel at His creation! Don't you make no never no mind. I may even speak at Chapel this night, if the spirit take me!'

'If the Devil don't take you, more like,' Mother said, for she liked to have the last word on a subject.

Father grabbed his special fossicking 'hoe' from by the door and then rummaged about in his sack of tools and handed me a tiny little hammer. I nearly threw it back at his feet, for it looked for all the world like something for a doll to me, but he caught the look in my eye and stayed my hand.

'You'll need it, Mary. Trust your old father. You'll see.'

I felt as proud as could be to be going on an adventure with Father. Just me!

We walked through the town with our shoulders hunched against the cold. We met few folk, it being Sunday, but I saw more than one nosy old biddy peek round her shutters and shake her head in disapproval. Father made no mind of them. We cut through the churchyard past St Michael the Archangel. Any moment those bells were going to start up again, trying to remind us where we should be on the Lord's Day but Father just started whistling in that jaunty way he had when he was off on an adventure. Father was a Dissenter. He didn't hold with the folk in St Michael's. Said they churchgoers were a lot of fancy folk who had forgotten about God and the Bible and were more interested in the rules made up by the church and that's why we went to Chapel where they put God and Jesus first instead of themselves.

'We'll be at Chapel right enough this very eve,' Father said, as if to reassure me but I was not in need of reassurance. The opinions of others mattered as little to me as they did to Father.

We walked over the turf to the path to Black Ven and Charmouth beyond. The sea lay to our right, a deep, forbidding grey. Sometimes it heaved like a great beast and spewed its foam onto the shore. Mostly it lurked as if it was in a sulk.

'Wind's going to get up a bit,' my father remarked. 'You scared, my little Mary? Scared 'bout what you've heard?'

'Not I!' I said, my words snatched by a gust of wind. 'I am on an adventure and I would not miss it for the world!'

'That's my girl! My Lightning Mary!'

He gave me a swift hug and we picked our way along the path for a few yards before he stopped again.

'Path's getting narrower by the day, Mary! Time was, you could walk side-be-side along here but see how it's fallen down onto the shore?'

He was right. I could see places where the ground had given way and gone tumbling down to the beach, taking the grass with it. The sea beast was dragging the land away into its giant mouth, dragging it in and spitting it out again.

'Will the path still be here when we turn back, Father?'

'Why?' he smiled. 'Are you afear'd? Do you want to turn for home now? It may be gone, tis true . . .'

'It would be an adventure if it was gone!'

He smiled again. 'You're a brave girl, my little lightning streak! Everything's an adventure to you, it seems! But your ma would roast me alive if anything happened to you!' He looked a bit sad, most likely thinking of the first Mary, who did get roasted.

It was slippery. You do have to watch your step. I was too young to understand then, but later I learned how dangerous it can be and I became anxious when Father went off on his own – and with good reason.

Of course, some folk end up in the sea by their own choice. Old Mr Cruickshanks used to go fossicking with Father, and when he ran out of money and couldn't even afford a bit of bread, he jumped off Gun Cliff and let the sea take him and his troubles. Mother said it could be Father doing that if he didn't get his cabinet-making done. Without that work – making furniture for rich folk – there'd be precious little money coming in from the sale of 'nonsenses', as she called them!

Besides, cabinet-making wasn't so very profitable in any event. Once a lady called Jane Austen called in at the workshop. She asked Father if he would give her a price to mend the broken lid of a box. He had to go round to her rooms to see it, for she was too grand to bring it to us. He gave her a fair price, five shillings, but she was too mean. She said that was more than all the chairs and tables were worth in the rented rooms! Father was most annoyed but he bit his tongue. She had no idea of the work involved to piece together the fragments and remake the little hinges! Father found out that she wrote books for rich ladies with nothing better to do than lie about reading nonsense and that she did not even put her own name on her books, so they must have been quite bad and maybe that was why she could not afford him.

Mother said he should have offered to lower his price, but Father wouldn't hear of it. He always said that if you charge nothing for your work, people think it's worth nothing. Mother muttered something about not telling him to mend it for *nothing*, but he wasn't listening. He had a trick to close his ears when Mother complained and I think I have that same trick myself. It is very useful.

It wasn't long before we reached Black Ven. To be truthful, it's a dirty grey more than black. Blue Lias clay, Father told me. Not really blue, neither, but the Lias bit is right, though. Layers and layers. (*Lias* means layers! Did you work that out?) Different shades of grey with some little seams of bright ochre and rust. A bit of grass clings to its sides. That day, what with the dark clouds hanging over us and the blackness of the rock, I could think it a devilish dark place indeed . . . and that set a little fizzle of excitement in my heart, I can tell you!

My father crouched down and took my face in his hands. 'Take a proper look at ol' Black Ven,' he said. 'It in't to be trusted. See this?' He pointed to a slab of dark, sludgy rock. 'That'll be off down the slope and into the sea before you can think the word *help*, let alone speak it. There used to be fields up there and cattle grazing on the sweet, green grass. All came toppling down one day. Cattle drowned. Farmer's life ruined. Lucky to be alive, himself. Used to be houses back along where we come, past the church. All gone. Swallowed by her.' He tilted his head towards the great green-grey sea. 'She's had a lot and she'll have more and she don't care whether she swallows cows or land or gardens or children. And the land can't be trusted to stay. It rushes to go back to her, to the sea . . . Won't hardly give you so much as a whisper of warning. You must understand, Mary, the land is cruel and the sea is cruel and life is cruel and that's the way it is.'

'Why do you come here, if it is so very cruel and dangerous?' I was frightened now, I will admit.

'Because of this!' He tapped a lump of clay. 'All because of this box of treasures.'

2

FROM THE MUD
COMES TREASURE

*F*ather tapped that lump of clay ever so gently. Then he just seemed to coax it and stroke it as if it was as frail as a wren's egg.

Gradually the mud fell away and I could see a stone in its centre like the pit in a plum. He took out his brush and swept away the last of the dust. Then he gave the stone a sharp little tap and it split in two, as if by magic. He held it out on his palm for me.

Curled up in the rock was the tiniest serpent you ever did see, with little stripes running all round its body. I could see little sparks of gold in it too. It looked alive, as if it might uncurl itself at any moment and wriggle away!

'Here,' said Father gently. 'Hold out your hand. This one's for you, little Mary. Your first treasure. You can keep it as a memento of your first treasure hunt with your old Pa.'

'It's beautiful!' I gasped, and I felt a fire catch hold in my head and my heart as I held the little thing.

'It'll be more so when I have had a polish of it.' Father smiled. 'You wait and see! It'll make a necklace fit for a queen! That's what we call a golden serpent, that is. T'in't real gold, but it's as like to real as makes no difference. Now, stow that away safe in your pocket, Mary, and take out that little hammer I gave you. I can't be doing all the work here!'

'But how do I know where to look?' I asked, for to be truthful, the mud and rocks looked all of a piece to me then, all the same as each other.

'You got to trust your instincts, Mary, and you got to be looking . . . really looking! If you want to find a curiosity, you got to be curious! See how this rock is all piled up like a heap of washing? Layers and layers? You have to look for anything that looks strange in there, see, where the beasts get trapped. A bit further down, you might find some ladies' fingers, nearer the foreshore. Or look for flat stones . . . but don't you try to split them without letting me see them first. There's a trick to it and if you get it wrong, you'll smash it to pieces.'

I stared at the cliff face and then I closed my eyes and pictured treasure in my hand and money in my pocket. Father was already collecting a heap of clay lumps and I began to do the same. My fingers were stiff from the cold and it was hard to get a grip. In future I would remember to put on my mittens.

My hand hovered over the rocks. I could not make up my

mind which to choose. I confess I made a little wish that I might find something exciting all by myself and make my father proud of me.

The first few lumps yielded nothing. They fell away under my hammer and left nothing behind. The next ten, twenty, thirty were the same, but Father seemed to be having more success. I saw him slip three or four pieces into his bag in what seemed like no time at all.

'You are so quick, Father!' I said, rather envious of the ease with which he seemed to find things.

'Quick?' he replied quizzically. 'Why, Mary, we have been here for more than the whole morning! See that pale sun and the sea so close? We don't have long before the sun will be off home to the West and the sea will be wetting our boots. We shall have to hurry home if we are to beat them both and be gettin' ourselves cleaned up for Chapel!'

He was right. The feeble sun, which could just be seen tinting the grey clouds ahead of us as we had walked to Black Ven, was now right above our heads. The sea was no more than two feet away. How had the time passed so swiftly?

Father had stopped work and was gathering up all his tools but I could not bear to think of going home without finding something by myself. I suddenly spotted a lump of rock the size of a goose egg. I seized it, tapped away at it and picked off lumps of clay with my frozen fingers. There, in the middle, was an oval stone, quite flat, about the length of my forefinger.

'Father! Could this be a curiosity?' I asked.

He stopped what he was doing and approached to take a look at what I had found. 'Why, do you think it might be, Mary?'

'I don't rightly know,' I said. 'I just feel it in my bones!'

'Bones, eh?' He winked at me. 'Bones to find bones, eh, Mary? Well, let's see if your bones are right!'

He gave the rock one of his sharp little taps and it fell in two, just like the one that had held my first treasure.

'Is there anything there?' I was so excited I could hardly breathe!

'Indeed there is, child!'

There, like a tiny chalky ghost, was a most curious creature, like nothing I had ever seen before.

'That's a scuttle you got there, Mary! He's like a cuttlefish. You've maybe never seen cuttlefish alive, but you've seen bits of them on the beach. Those white, feather-light things that look like a petal ... the things the birds seem to like so much.'

My first find! A scuttle! I hid it in my pocket with my first treasure. I felt so happy that I could have skipped about for joy but for the strange feeling that the ground beneath my feet might slip away if I disturbed it.

Father finished packing away his tools. He looked at the sky, which had turned a sullen grey, grim clouds covering the setting sun.

'Right! Best be heading home now,' he said. 'Weather's closing in and it'll be dark soon. We don't want to be stranded now, do we? And we don't want to be getting a scolding from your ma! She'll be worriting!' He gave my cheek a pinch. 'Got that colour in 'em, like I promised,' he chuckled.

'When can we come here again?' I asked.

'That's my girl! We can come just as soon as I have finished that desk. Sooner I am paid for that work, the better. With the price of corn these days, tis a job to put bread on the table. These little findings of ours won't fetch much this time of year. Not so many fancy folk visiting. Still, we'll have a store of treasures ready come the spring, won't we, Mary?'

'Maybe we'll find a big treasure, Father?' I said, in a hopeful way.

'Don't see why not! With you and Joseph and me all hunting together? I'd say it were as good as found!'

3

LEARNING THE TRADE

*S*ummer was the best time for selling, but winter was far and away the best for finding. Those storms throw the earth about, revealing treasures and then, just as quick, hiding them again. You have to be out there all weathers if you want to find things. But it's mighty dangerous.

The tide can come in while you aren't watching and the sea will sweep you up and carry you off. The ground beneath your feet can be snatched away in an instant. Worse still, the ground above you can come tumbling down and bury you deep, where no one would find you until the sea carried the mud and rocks away again . . . and then it would be too late.

You were not even safe in your own home. When I was a very small child, the sea rose up in a rage one night and hurled all manner of stones and such against our house. The water poured in – a great torrent – and sucked away the whole staircase as it left, leaving us all stranded upstairs. I scarce remember it, but Joseph could recount the whole story of how we were all rescued through the bedroom window at dawn and Mother often spoke of the destruction visited upon us by the sea.

But the sea, for all she can be a monster, is also the treasure-seeker's friend. She can wash stuff clean so you can see it and she can bring down curiosities from high above where you'd never hope to reach them otherwise. Without the sea to pull apart those layers, we'd have slim pickings indeed. We thank her in our hearts, but fear her too.

Father took Joseph and me on his expeditions whenever he could. We were even out on Christmas Day with our baskets and hammers. There wasn't a muffler knitted could keep out the cold and Joseph and I had to fight to keep our teeth from chattering after Father joked that the noise and the rattling would bring the cliff down on top of us! We worked as hard and as fast as we could for the few hours of light the good Lord gave us but the luck I had had when I had first searched with Father seemed to have abandoned me. Most of what we found was what Father called 'ornery' but it would earn us a few coins come the spring and anything was better than nothing, as he rightly said.

Mother despaired. 'What are you thinking of, Richard, to risk the lives of the only two children left to us? And on Christmas Day too!' she wailed.

'But we want to go with Father!' piped up Joseph. 'It's interesting! It's good for us to be out!'

Seemed Mother wasn't the only one to think we should bide at home. One day that winter, a woman we'd never seen before, new to Lyme maybe, came up to Father and poked him in the chest with her walking stick. She must have been spying on us for she seemed to have her mind and her opinions quite made up.

'You ought to be ashamed of yourself!'

Father was bewildered. 'Why?' he asked. 'What have I done that I should be ashamed of? I can think of nothing. Do you have the right man?'

'Indeed I do!' she growled back at him. 'These children are nothing but servants to you! Why, if they were slaves in the New World, you could not treat them worse! You daily risk their lives and for what? To line your own miserable pocket!'

And with that she gave him an extra hard jab with the stick and marched off up Broad Street, muttering as she went.

Father stood, dazed, for a moment. 'Well, do I make you my little slaves?' he asked. 'Do you feel mistreated by your old father?'

'No, no!' we cried, for we would sooner be in our graves than miss our adventures on the cliffs.

I loved to be out there with him. All weathers. I knew he would have been out there morning, noon and night but his cabinet work took him away for days at a time, making some fancy piece of furniture for folks with money to burn but still too mean to pay what's fair.

'You must make hay while the sun shines,' Mother always said when he got what she called proper work. He muttered and looked black as thunder but he knew it had to be done.

We had to be grateful to the nose-in-the-air highborn folk at every turn. The sun brought out all manner of fancy types from Bath and London. Prancing about in the Assembly Rooms. Picking their way around the town and holding their noses down at the quayside and grimacing at the boxes of the fancy fish that only they could afford to eat while we had the leavings. Dressed up in silks and frills, whether they were men or women, and looking as silly as could be to my mind. What was the use of a pale pink dress if it was trailing in the mud? What was the use of a bonnet with ribbons and feathers if it got snatched away by the wind? If I had to choose between fine clothes and a fine adventure, I'd choose adventure any day.

Of course, I had no such choice and the plain truth was that when the summer brought these silly creatures into Lyme by the carriage-load, that's when Father could sell some of his curiosities and make enough money to keep Mother happy for a while. He was quite well known and folk came from miles to see what was on his little table in front of the workshop. Joseph and I were proud to see our own finds laid out for them to gawp at. Of course, those folk in all their finery had to keep their gloves on to touch anything, so scared were they of a bit of dust or dirt, poor creatures!

At least they were a bit more sensible than the mad people who came to Lyme in the winter months. Those poor souls followed the advice of a certain Dr Crane of Weymouth who advised bathing in the sea in January and February for its 'benefits to health'! How I used to laugh at the sight of them, taking off their clothes in the bitter cold and rushing across the stones, yelping like puppies, and on into the grey water, screaming with pain as it turned their bodies blue and then red as any boiled lobster. They didn't stay in long, I can tell you, and as for it being a cure for all ills and the secret to good health? Well, all I can say is that more went home in a box on the back of a cart than in a carriage, so a fat lot of good all that freezing water did them. I could have told them straight off that it was a fool's errand and I would have charged them a lot less than any doctor for that advice. I do wonder where people's brains are sometimes.

I did not have much regard for those people as a rule, it is true, but there was one encounter which was a pleasure to be remembered always. My first real trade, when I was no more than eight years old. An old gentleman picked up a tiny little ram's horn I had found and which Father had polished so that it shone in the sunshine. My heart thumped in my chest as I watched the old gentleman turn it over and over in his hand, staring at it in wonder.

As I watched him, my hand went to the snakestone that hung from a leather strip around my neck. It was the one Father had found for me on my first visit to Black Ven. He had split it down the middle, polished both faces of the stone and put a hole in near the snake's head for the leather. It gleamed a rich golden brown when it caught the sun and maybe it was a good-luck charm too, for the old gentleman seemed to catch a glimpse of it before he spoke again.

'I'll give you twopence for this,' he said, holding out the coins.

'Sixpence!' The words were out of my mouth before I'd had a moment to think. Father looked at me as if he did not believe what he had just heard and, truth to tell, it should not have been more than three pennies at the most.

'That's a lot of money, young lady, for a bit of old stone,' said the old gentleman.

'It's not a bit of old stone,' said I. 'It's a treasure and I risked my life to fetch it out of the treacherous mud of Black Ven so rich folk like you can gaze on it.'

The old man laughed. He seemed kind enough, not like some of them London types with their airs and graces. He turned to Father. 'Your daughter drives a hard bargain, but she's understood the importance of provenance.'

'What's provenance? Don't you mean providence?' I replied. It was a bit cheeky to talk back at a gentleman but I like to know the meaning of words.

He smiled again. 'Provenance is all about where things come from, my dear. Here's your sixpence. Now *that* is providence! May it buy you a good dinner for you and your family. She's a credit to you, sir. A brave little wench!'

He pocketed the ram's horn and tipped his hat at me. I thought my heart would burst. My first sale in front of Father. He could see how good I should prove at commerce!

Father ruffled my hair, laughing all the while. 'Well, my little Lightning Mary. You'll be taking over from your old pa in no time at all. We'll be rich!'

But we weren't. Nor never like to be so with the meanness of most of our customers. They picked over stuff, tutting at prices, and my outspoken ways did not always work the same magic with them. Father, on the other hand, could charm a bird out of a tree if he had a mind to and between us we sold enough to buy bread and milk and even meat.

'These rich folk, Mary, they'll beat you down at every turn! You got to stand your ground. Look them in the eye and don't take any of their nonsense. It's the only way and don't you forget it! But hark at me! I'm telling the toughest little saleswoman in all of Dorset!'

He would always ruffle my hair when he praised me. It was just about the only touch I could ever bear.

4

A SALE AND A SPY

I was never one for toys or dolls. After my hammer, my snakestone necklace was my most prized possession. It was a comfort to me to stroke it as I shut my eyes and imagined myself somewhere on the beach, alone or with Father, finding curiosities amongst the seaweed, mud and stones.

The children at Sunday School mocked me, as they always did:

> *'Mary Anning got no bread!*
> *All she's got is a stone instead!*
> *Mary, Mary! Can't eat stones!*
> *Never mind, she'll chew on bones!'*

They thought themselves so clever with their rhymes. I reckon they were jealous of my treasure.

It was true that we did not have much food. Nobody did, except the farmers' children. Why those invading Frenchies would ever want to come here I never did understand, for most of the time there wasn't much in Lyme more than mud and babies dying and folk scraping along, best they could. Leastways, in the winter months.

One Sunday in March, not two months before my tenth birthday, I went on Black Ven by myself, after school. I ignored the girls who asked me where I was going. I pretended not to hear the taunts and jeers of the boys. I put them all behind me as I raced round the streets and onto the path behind the church.

I just had a feeling that I was going to be lucky, going to find something really big or really beautiful or both, and nobody was going to stop me.

I thought I'd find a treasure really quickly – and I did! A big lump of clay seemed to be waiting for me in my path. A few pushes and prods with my fingers to prise the mud away and there was a rock as big as a gull's egg and just as smooth. Two sharp taps of my hammer and there was one of the finest ram's horns I ever did see. I whooped with joy and then looked around to check no one had heard me. Not that I really expected anyone to be there, as Joseph was helping Father in the workshop and nobody else was inclined to fossicking ever since old Cruickshanks had jumped into the sea. Yet, out of the corner of my eye, I caught a movement and then I saw a head of blond curls ducking down behind a rock.

'Come out!' I cried. 'Show yourself! I know you are there!'

But the figure did not come out. Instead, I heard footsteps, gradually getting fainter as my spy ran away from me.

'Coward!' I shouted, quite proud to have frightened the intruder away.

I returned to my find. How splendid it looked, curled and ridged like the finest twisty horn you will ever see on a sheep itself.

There's many as believe exactly what it says in the Bible: that God created this whole world and everything that is in it all in just six days. Father said that couldn't be. He said learned folk had worked out that days meant something else, and that it was six thousand years not days. But he also said he had heard that others were beginning to talk of many times that number. 'As much as seventy-five thousand!' Father said, though it was hard for me to imagine how much time that was, for even a day in my life passed slowly sometimes.

We only talked of these matters on the beach or cliffs, where we could not be heard, because there were people who would have said Father's thoughts were the Devil's work and against the truth in the Good Book. There are many things I could not understand (and still cannot) and which made me think that not everything in the Bible was completely true. It says God created everything at once, but why have some things vanished? Why don't we find live snakestones and scuttles? Why create a thing and then make no more of it? Especially something so beautiful. Makes no sense to me.

And where are all the bones of men and horses and sheep and the like in the rocks? We only find those on the beach when the sea washes them up and she's only had them long enough to feed the fishes and wash the bones clean as a peeled potato. They haven't been buried deep in the earth as these curiosities have been. So did the rocks split open to fit the treasures in? How? It's a mystery.

I stroked the treasure and then took it down to the water to wash off the last of the mud. It was as big as the palm of my hand.

I was lost in wonder.

Then a wave of fear passed through me. The sun had dipped. The sea was menacing up the shoreline, snapping her great jaws at my ankles. I was late. Maybe too late!

I ran for all I was worth, clutching my prize. Up and down the slippery path, clambering up the bank into the churchyard, pleased to feel solid earth beneath my feet. As I rounded the last gravestone, I smacked straight into the billowing skirts of a lady and dropped my treasure! Dropped it on her foot!

She gave a little yelp but I also heard another sound. A snigger. A little stifled laugh. I looked round, furious and no doubt red with embarrassment. Who was laughing at me?

'Mercy me, child! You *are* in a rush!' said the lady, in kind tones.

'Begging pardon, mistress,' I muttered, staring all the while at her feet.

'Now! What have we here?' The lady stooped to pick up my find. 'Well, well! What a pretty thing! Where did you get this?' she asked.

I looked up at her. A grand lady, no doubt about that. Quite young. Clothes that must have cost a pretty penny. A grave expression on her face, which I thought mighty suitable since we were in the churchyard.

'I didn't steal it,' says I, as I snatched it back from her.

'Did I say that you did?' she returned, with a smile on her lips and in her eyes. She seemed kind enough.

'I found it. Back there. On Black Ven. Don't you be like to go and look there, though. Tis too dangerous for the likes of you. And' – here I looked at her very pretty leather shoes – 'very muddy. Very muddy indeed. And the tide's coming in.'

She laughed. 'What a funny creature you are! I have no mind to risk my life *or* my shoes, I can assure you. But I do have a mind to own this pretty thing. How much will you take for it? A shilling?' She stared intently at me. 'Ah, I see by your face that a shilling will not do it. Half a crown, then? Will that persuade you?'

Half a crown! I could see in a flash that this lady's half-crown could work all sorts of magic. First, it would buy some much-needed food; second, it would make my father proud; third, it would make Joseph jealous; and last and best of all, it would buy me peace from Mother, who would have been like to give me such a hiding for going to Black Ven in the first place but could scarce punish me now.

'I'll let you have it for that sum,' I said. 'But only because it dropped on your foot and I am sorry. Otherwise it would be five shillings.'

An audible gasp came from the bushes and I looked sharply in their direction.

The lady seemed not to have heard this interruption to our dealings. She laughed again, in a quite unladylike fashion, her head thrown back and her white teeth flashing, before reaching into her little silk pouch and drawing out the large silver coin that would be the ransom due my mother.

'Here you are, child. You are quite the little business-woman! You'll go far, I am sure!'

'Father could split it in two and polish it . . . like this one.' I pulled out my treasure from under my scarf and showed her.

'Oh no, I like it just as it is. True to itself. Just as the Lord made it and you found it.'

'I doubt it was this dead stone when the Lord made it,'

said I. 'Must have been a creature in it, like a snail or some such.'

'Nevertheless, I shall enjoy it as it is. Thank you. Who are you, child?'

'Mary. Mary Anning. The first Mary was burned up in a fire. I am nearly ten. I was struck by lightning and survived.' I don't know why I told her all that, but it seemed to amuse her.

'My! What a story, Mary! No wonder you are such a spirited thing! Take care that that spirit of yours does not lead you into danger!' With that she patted me on the head rather as if I was a dog (which made me somewhat vexed) and was gone.

'Now, villain!' I turned my attention to the bush. 'Come out this instant!'

That very same blond hair appeared, atop a pink and white face that betokened some rich child accustomed to much soap and water. A boy in a blue velvet jacket. Older than me by two, maybe three years, but still a boy. Wide-eyed as a rabbit or a mackerel. He stood gawping, open-mouthed as any idiot. And then he fled. Again.

'Coward!' I shouted, for the second time that day.

I should have felt a little cowardly myself as I sneaked in the back door and took off my muddy boots.

Mother was in the kitchen, peeling turnips, her face as black as thunder.

'And where've you been, miss?' She slammed the blade of the knife down on a poor turnip as if she'd like to murder it.

I held out the coin. It shone like a mirror. It shone like something magic, because Mother's face cleared like the sky over the Cobb when the dark clouds are chased away by the wind and the blue returns.

Then the thunder was back.

'Where'd you get that, then?'

I felt a little thrill of pride and defiance go through me.

'Sold a treasure! Sold a treasure of my own finding.'

'Have you no shame to be doing business on the Sabbath?' Mother thundered.

'I had quite forgot and so had the lady. A great lady. She did not mind at all. She was very pleased and she said that I would go far!'

'Oh, you'll go far, all right,' retorted Mother. 'Far out to sea and into Davy Jones's locker. Tis your father's fault! I knew he should never have taken 'e to Black Ven and given 'e a taste for it. There'll be tragedy. You mark my words!'

'Not tragedy . . . just treasure! Half a crown, Mother! Now is that a tragedy? Tomorrow, shall I go and buy a bit of mutton for our tea? I'm good at bargaining.'

Mother could not help smiling, though I could tell she was fighting to stay fierce. 'Very well. Maybe that customer of yours was right! But when you go, mind you don't get distracted by any treasures on your way! There isn't a scrap of mutton to be found on Black Ven, is there, madam? And don't you go telling me of sheep fallen over the cliff, neither. Now. Make yourself useful and clean all that mud off the front step.'

The next day we had a mutton stew as tasty as you like and all thanks to me and my treasure. I was indulging in the sin of pride and did I care? I did not!

My pleasure was short-lived. As we washed and dried our bowls, Joseph started nudging me in the ribs and winking. It seemed my own brother was a spy himself. When Mother was distracted, he hissed in my ear, 'You've got an admirer!'

I was about to give him a good dig with my elbow but he just laughed and went outside, forcing me to follow him to find out what he knew.

He said he had seen my spy following me around like a lovesick spaniel and then he started to talk all sorts of nonsense which I tried with all my might to ignore. Did I like the velvet finery? Was I taken with the boy's golden curls? Did I want to kiss him? As Joseph well knew, I never had time for fancy clothing and have always thought that boys in silk and frills look even sillier than the girls. And as for kissing – ugh! I gave Joseph a thump for his talk of kissing and told him I neither knew nor cared about the creature who hid in bushes and spied on me and knew nothing whatever about him.

I made my fiercest face at Joseph and drew my finger across my throat as Mother came out to see why we were neglecting our chores.

Joseph just smiled and winked again.

Boys are so annoying!

5

HOW TO CATCH A SPY

*D*id I really know nothing about the mystery boy? I knew from his uniform that he was at the school for young gentlemen way up the hill, away from the stink of the nets and the lobster pots. It had crossed my mind that he might have wanted to take away my treasures – or the money I'd been making from them – but why would a rich boy have need of my few pennies? Besides, there was no means to discover what he intended because every time I caught him spying on me, he ran away. He was a coward. No doubt about it.

Or mad.

I determined to catch him and make him speak to me. He was older than me, that much was clear, so he should have been the braver but he wasn't. What a chicken! Did I have three heads? Did I breathe fire like a dragon? I did not. What fun it would have been if I could, though! Imagine!

I had to set a trap.

*

I thought about how to confront him all the time I was awake. Joseph tapped the side of his nose and winked at me every time I caught his eye. It made me very cross indeed to think that he might be able to read my mind.

Sunday came, and I found it hard to concentrate on schoolwork when, in my head, I was working out how to catch the creature.

I was sitting next to Hettie Bowditch. She was pink-faced and yellow-haired, not unlike my spy. I could hear her humming away as she made her letters slowly, slowly, her tongue sticking out between her teeth and the tune of a dance coming out of her nose, seemingly. It was the first warm day of spring and a huge bluebottle fly, its body as shiny as a piece of sea glass, kept crashing into the window, too stupid to find a way out, its noisy buzzing mixing with Hettie's humming. It fair made my head explode.

'How in the world is a person to *think*!'

Most unfortunately, that thought came out and out loud without me even realising I'd said it.

Miss Evans, the schoolmistress, looked up from her book in alarm and then displeasure. 'Mary Anning! Cease your interrupting!'

'I *have* ceased,' I said, for I was no longer speaking and, therefore, no longer 'interrupting' (as she would have it) when she bade me stop. Some people speak no sense and they speak it more often than not, in my opinion.

'Out! Out! You rude child!'

The whole class started to snigger, and then to giggle and then to laugh out loud. Miss Evans went redder than the reddest gurnard. (That's a fish, if you didn't know.)

'I don't understand, miss,' said I, for, in truth, I did not understand why she had become so cross. 'I only said but a few words and ceased before you felt obliged to tell me.'

'Wilful child! Will you answer me back?'

'I will if you wish it!' I replied and, really, I could not for the life of me fathom out what she wanted, as she was very far from being logical and I was too busy with my plan to have the time to work her out.

Miss Evans strode towards me, cutting a passage through the little gap between the desks, knocking Billy Stickland's slate off and stepping on Andrew Hallett's foot. She ignored his squeak. Her face was as dark as Black Ven itself.

On reaching my desk, she grabbed me forcibly by the arm and marched me out of the room. 'You can return to the classroom when you have mended your manners. Be thankful that this is your only punishment and let it be a warning to you.'

She slammed the door and left me with my thoughts.

I quickly realised that I would not be mending my

manners that afternoon since I had not broken them in the first place. Miss Evans had done me a great injustice but she had done me an even greater favour, for I could now spend the rest of the day setting a trap for my spy!

It was tricky enough to get past Mother when she was at home busy with a baby. It was even trickier when she had no baby to distract her. There was but one door, and even if I could get through that unnoticed, the stairs creaked like a ship breaking up in a storm and Mother had the ears of a hare.

I knew enough to be sure that Mother would not think I had done the best thing by escaping school, but I couldn't even make up a story about it to please her for I cannot lie. I simply can't. Father and Joseph berated me many times for my truth-telling when they would have me cover up their mischief with a lie. They had a habit of forgetting that I cannot do anything but tell the truth.

Once, Joseph begged me to say that I had seen him slip over and split his nose when I had seen him fighting with Ethan Coombs . . . and beating him, I might add. Mother took a dim view of fighting and Joseph was in fear of the consequence.

'How did you come to be in this state?' she asked, as she scrubbed the blood from his face.

'Slipped and fell, Ma. Mary saw me, didn't you, Mary?'

'Well, Mary? Is your brother telling the truth?' Mother demanded.

Joseph turned his puppy-dog eyes on me, wide and watery as any grand lady's spaniel. He mouthed the word '*please*' but it was no good. The truth will always out . . . when it comes out of my mouth anyway.

'He is not. He made fun of Ethan, and then Ethan punched him on the nose and then Joseph punched him so hard that Ethan lost his senses. And Joseph won,' I added, confident that that would make everything all right.

'Mary!' shouted Joseph in exasperation. 'Can you never help your poor brother out?'

Mother growled at him. 'If you told the truth in the first place, there'd be no need to call on Mary. Your father will have something to say about this, Joseph. I'm ashamed of you! Brawling! At your age! Here, you can peel these potatoes. Not that you'll be eating any of them, mind.'

Joseph pinched me hard on the arm but I did not squeak nor did I tell Mother what he did for she never asked me. I won't be a telltale if I'm not asked but I cannot help but tell the truth if I am.

Father said there is such a thing as a white lie for when you get asked a question and it would be rude or hurtful to give a truthful answer, but I cannot do that either. So, if

Mother asked us if we were enjoying our supper, I could not help but say that I was not and was only eating it because I must eat something and there was nothing else. This did not make Mother happy. She told me that if I could not think of anything nice to say, I should say nothing at all, so I was mostly silent, which quite suited me. A lot of talk just fills up space and is of no use whatsoever.

Anyway, there I was at the door, knowing full well that I couldn't sneak past Mother and couldn't lie to her if she asked me why I was not at school; so it was best to get it over and done with.

It was quiet as the grave in the house. No pots bubbling away. No cross mutterings from Mother as she cleaned or washed or mended clothes. She was not at home. What a piece of luck!

I found my hammer and then collected up my little sack of curiosities. I was going to need them for my trap! It would be worth parting with a few to catch my spy.

I was waiting to hear the coward's footsteps behind me until I realised that it was too early in the day. My spy would still be sitting at a table, sticking his silver knife and fork into the finest roast beef or capon or spooning up a posset. I could feel my excitement at catching him vanishing like a sea mist. I had a plan and now it made no sense to put it into action.

45

I had set a trail of treasures, but now it might have been found and taken by others *and* I would have had to wait so long and it would have been so very dull. I never like a change in plans and even the thought of a spell of treasure-hunting was not enough to lift my spirits. I began to remove my carefully-laid trail.

There was a freshly dug grave, all the earth piled up in a great heap and I stopped to read the name on the little wooden cross. Amy Martin. She was not known to me. Seventeen years old. No doubt it was the wasting disease took her off. Or maybe childbirth. A shiver ran down my spine. I should be more than halfway through my life if I were to die when she did. How little time that would be. Too little time to waste trying to catch a silly spy too chicken to show his face. I gathered up the last of my treasures from the path.

'I'm not *that* stupid! I know you don't find such things lying on the grass!'

The voice behind me made me jump near clean out of my skin and I dropped two Devil's toenails in my fright.

I wheeled round, making my face as fierce and as furious as I could. 'How dare you! How *dare* you sneak up on a body! In a graveyard!' I shouted, before I realised who I was shouting at.

My spy!

He was laughing. That is something I will not tolerate. I charged at him like an angry bull, hitting him full in the chest with my head and knocking him down.

He stopped laughing as he fell. He flailed his arms instead, but they could not stop him. There was a nasty thud when he hit the ground and, as he did so, he closed his eyes. It all happened so quickly and so slowly at the same time.

I've killed him.

That was the first thought that came into my head. He had struck his head so hard that he was dead.

I have killed him. I have killed a rich boy who did me no harm beyond annoying me and I have killed him stone dead.

I would be deported or hanged, for sure!

6
FRENCH HENRY,
WHO ISN'T FRENCH

I was standing over the body of a rich boy. A rich boy I'd killed.

His face was pale as a seagull's chest. His hair was fanned out like a mermaid's curls.

I didn't know what to do.

Then the body started to shake. The eyes crinkled at their edges. The shoulders started to jump up and down and then a massive snort, like to that of a pig, burst out of his nose.

His eyes opened. Very blue. He sat up and started picking grass out of his hair.

'Fooled you! Ah! Revenge! So sweet!'

Did I tell you that I do not like to be made fun of? Well, I do not. Not at all. I was minded to hit him again. Really hard this time. He saw the fury on my face and smiled, holding out his white hand.

'Henry De la Beche, at your service, ma'am. Go on! Shake!'

'I'll never shake a Frenchie's hand,' said I, and no more I would. Everyone had heard the tales from the war with old Boney Bonaparte who called himself Emperor and was about three feet high and we were all reminded nearly every day to keep a lookout for spies who sneaked onto our shores in the dead of night, pretending to be fisherfolk or our own sailors.

He got up and dusted himself down. 'I'm as English as you are. My family goes back generations in England.'

'Sounds French to me! And you sneak! You sneak around and hide yourself. You hide yourself and then you run away. You *are* a spy! A coward and a spy!'

'Neither, I assure you.'

'Then why are you always following me? Sneaking and peeking and running away? Watching what I'm doing? Sounds just like spying to me!'

He shrugged his shoulders. 'I'm sorry. I'm a bit shy. And you are always so busy . . . digging or dealing.'

'So you admit that you were watching me sell my ram's horn to that lady! No doubt you thought to steal my findings or my money!'

'No! No. I am just very interested in what you are doing. Fascinated, really, and . . .'

'And what?' I tried to sound as fierce as I could.

He pushed his hair out of his eyes and looked straight

49

at me. 'I hoped you might let me help you. Come with you. Obviously, I'd have a lot to learn from you. You are so clearly an expert in this field. I am just an ignorant boy.'

'Well, you've got that bit right. You are certainly ignorant,' I said stoutly; but I had to admit that it was quite pleasing to be asked for help by one so much older and grander. 'I learned all I know from my father. Why can't your father teach you?'

A strange look passed over his face. He seemed like to cry. Still a cowardly baby, then!

'My father is dead.'

'How?'

He looked at me sharply, almost angrily. 'You should not ask such things.'

'But why? I want to know, and only you can tell me.'

He sighed and sat down on the edge of a grave and then leaped off it as it if had burned his backside. I really thought he would cry then.

'We don't speak of it. My mother and I. We never speak of it.' He *was* crying, his face becoming red and blotchy.

Again, I found myself not knowing what to do. A boy should not be crying. Joseph would never cry.

He wiped his face with a large handkerchief. I was still waiting for his explanation and maybe he could see that I was getting a little impatient for he muttered, between sniffs,

'You aren't a very agreeable person, are you? For a girl, especially.'

'And you aren't a very brave person, are you? For a boy, especially,' I retorted, quick as you like. 'Besides, who says girls have to be agreeable?'

He gave an almighty sniff and rubbed his eyes furiously before saying, 'And who says boys must always be brave? I hope, for your sake, that you never have to lose your father.'

'Well, that is quite the silliest thing anyone could say! My father will not live for ever. Nothing does. Crying won't bring your father back. Mother cries over the dead babies for days but none of them ever come back. Dead is dead. Nothing to be done but get on with living.'

'You're a hard creature. Hard as your "treasures".'

I let this pass. 'So how did he die?' I asked.

Father said I was like a dog with a bone sometimes and at that moment I did not feel at all inclined to let this bone drop. Persistent is what I am and always will be.

Henry's face was reddened with anger now, not tears.

'If you must know, he died of fever. In Jamaica. Our first visit to our plantation. He fell ill and then he died. He died a horrible death, wracked by pain. He spewed his guts up. He writhed in agony in his bed. He burned up with a fever. And then he died! Happy now? Oh, and it might also entertain you to know that my mother and I were shipwrecked and

51

nearly drowned on our voyage back to England. There! Is that enough tragedy for you?'

I was impressed. His father's death sounded very normal to me, but to be in a shipwreck and live to tell the tale was a very interesting thing indeed! I had to know more! Henry, it seemed, could read minds, because he started to speak again.

'I see that has got your attention, you fiend. Maybe you would also care to imagine how it feels to be robbed of your father, to see your mother spend her days crying, not eating, growing thinner and paler and then to have to leave your father behind in his grave and set sail and then—' He stopped to blow his nose again. 'Then to be caught in the most terrifying of storms, tossed about on waves as high as a cliff and then dashed on a coral reef with five other ships. The sea was full of bodies, bodies cut to ribbons by the coral, and we and the other poor souls who survived left clinging to the rocks, watching as sharks feasted on the dead and dying.'

This was quite the most exciting story I had heard since Noah's Flood and that was not so very interesting as there were no accounts of sharks eating the wicked who did not have a place on the Ark. Henry could see the gleam of excitement in my eye for he continued, and I fancied he was beginning to forget to be sad for there was a light in his own red-rimmed eyes.

'Your blood would have frozen in your veins if you had heard the cries of the men as they tried to defend themselves against the mighty sharks with their great teeth and thrashing tails. The sea was red as any sunset. Red with blood. I saw heads and hands and limbs washed up by the tide. I saw great seabirds peck out the eyes and gorge upon the flesh. I saw sailors retch their innards up or soil their nether garments from terror at the sight. I saw—'

'Enough!' I had begun to feel ever so slightly sick myself. 'How came you to be rescued, then? Or is this tale a web of lies?'

He blushed a little. 'Well, maybe there weren't so many sharks, but men really were cut to ribbons on the coral; and this I swear is true: the sailors would have eaten me and a little girl also saved, if it wasn't for the Commodore hearing of our plight and sending a ship to rescue us.'

'*Eat* you!' I exclaimed.

'Yes! Eat us! They were like ravenous wolves. They eyed us up like pies on a shelf. One of them pinched my arm to see how much meat was on it. My mother flew at him and he backed away but we were this far' – he held up his finger and thumb just a hair's breadth apart – 'from having our throats slit and our bodies roasted over hot stones!'

'Ugh! Disgusting!'

'Ha! Not so brave now, are you?' he crowed triumphantly.

53

'Oh, I am not scared by your tale. I just think you would have tasted disgusting.'

In truth, I was rather horrified. I could imagine hunger well enough. I had felt it often. But a hunger that would drive you to eat another person? I shuddered to think of it.

Henry De la Beche was watching me closely, as if waiting for me to say more.

'Well, that's a fine story and perhaps we have something in common, for I am myself the survivor of a storm,' I said, 'and it does explain why you cannot learn from your father, him being dead.' I saw him wince a bit at these words but the truth is the truth. 'But how am I to profit from teaching you is what I should like to know?'

He reached into his pocket and brought out a small notebook. 'Here.' He offered it to me and I undid the ribbon that was keeping its pages tight closed.

It was full of drawings. Drawings of plants, of birds, of dogs and cats and, of more interest to me, stones. They were good. Faithful reproductions of the subjects. They looked alive or real. He had a skill I did not possess, that was clear.

I could feel him watching me, waiting for a reaction. I handed him back his book and hid my delight behind a stern countenance, not unlike my mother's when she feigns displeasure but she is secretly pleased with me.

'Very well. You could be useful, but all the drawings you

make for me shall have their own book, is that understood? I won't have the treasures muddled up with cats and flowers.'

He grinned at me and raised his hand to his head in salute. 'Understood. At your command, Captain . . . Captain?'

'Miss Anning will suffice. Good day to you, Frenchie. We will commence work tomorrow.'

And with that, I left him where he stood, smiling fit to burst.

7

MY FIRST REAL FRIEND

I did not tell Father about Henry, and Joseph seemed to have grown weary of teasing me. Besides, he had started work as an apprentice to the upholsterer and was too busy learning how to make puffed-up cushioned settles for the precious bottoms of the rich, so I was left alone in my endeavours. Or not quite alone, now.

I have always preferred to be alone above all else, but the truth is that I did feel a bit safer out there on the shifting ground at the foot of Black Ven when Henry was there too. Would God have spared him from being eaten by the sharks or the cannibal sailors only to have him caught and killed in a landfall? He may have been my lucky charm and, perhaps, I was his, for he did seem to be of a sunnier disposition than when first I met him.

When his summer holidays began, he came out with me almost every day. It amused me that what was work for me was a holiday for him. Maybe being in school every day instead of just Sunday would have been a holiday for me.

He had his faults. The worst was that he was easily distracted. One hot, July day, another French-sounding gentleman, very elderly, calling himself Mr De Luc (from Switzerland, Henry said) stopped to say good day. Of course, he did not speak to me though I could have told him a thing or two. Instead, he passed two hours or more studying the rocks and discussing with Henry what the layers might be and how they got there. I could see well enough that the sea helped make them the way they are, for I observed every day how she took things away and brought old and new things back again and piled them up. It was my belief that she found and uncovered creatures that had lived a very long time ago but were no more and that meant that Time was important too.

On the window ledge at home, there was a dead wasp that had been buried under dust and sand and leaves and more dust, and those layers were just like the layers in the rock. I knew the wasp was still there because I kept lifting up the layers to see what was happening to its body and there it was – a papery thing with all its juices dried up, but there nonetheless. If that body can be buried under all that matter, what creatures might there be in the cliffs?

The Swiss gentleman talked and talked – quite like a preacher, if you ask me. I could only hear snatches of his 'sermon' as I worked. He used a lot of mighty long words and Henry, to my mind, pretended to understand all he said. Maybe he really did.

Henry had made some drawings of the face of Black Ven and the Swiss gentleman liked them very much. I thought to myself that if he sold them to the gentleman, then I should get some payment. It stood to reason as it was only because I knew the paths and the tides that he could be out here safely, sketching away under my protection.

But he didn't offer to sell them, and when the Swiss gentleman turned to walk back to Charmouth, Henry's eyes were shining with excitement.

'He was much taken with my drawings and he has given me the most marvellous idea! I shall make a book showing the geology of our isles!' he said.

'Geology?' How I hated to show him that I did not know the meaning of the word, for I always expected a rich boy such as he to take any opportunity to tease me for being ill-educated and ignorant.

As usual, I was wrong to fear this. Henry was kind. He *is* kind. I should always remember that.

'The study of rocks. It's the scientific word, Miss Anning. From the Greek! "Geo" means Earth and the "ology" bit comes from a word, "logia", meaning "the study of". So, geology means the study of the Earth and a geologist is someone who studies the Earth. *You* are a geologist! A scientist!'

I could barely hide the surge of pride at these words but I felt some alarm too. 'Hush! Do not talk of science to folk round here!' I warned him. 'You'll bring God's wrath down upon your head! Or the wrath of the townsfolk.'

'But many of your customers are scientists, and *you* are a scientist yourself!' Henry seemed baffled. How little he really knows!

'No, I am not and never say that I am. I am a treasure-hunter. I hunt for money not for knowledge. As to our customers, it is none of our business why they be interested in our wares. It is a matter of trade for us. We must struggle to make money where we can. We do not all live like you, Frenchie.'

Henry blushed. He blushed very easily. He was ashamed to be rich. I liked him for that.

'I am sorry that money is so hard-earned, Miss Anning. Maybe there are safer ways for you to get it?'

'Piffle! What do I care for safety? Besides,' said I, ''tis better to be treasure-hunting than selling all your hair like poor Fanny Goodfellow.' And it was! Much better.

'Selling hair? Why would you sell your hair?' He looked confused as any rich person might who has no idea of how

59

we struggle, or maybe it was just that I had gone from science to trade to hair. It is how my mind works. I see connections.

I told him how poor Fanny had the most beautiful long curls, the colour of ripe corn, but they had all been cut off by the barber and cut off so close to her poor skull that the skin was quite red and raw in places. They rubbed oil all over her bare head but it still stung like fury, Fanny said. She had to wear a scratchy woollen cap all through the winter, and for weeks after it was cut off she still had nothing but a few hairs poking through, like shoots of grass in the snow. Her hair was sold to pay for firewood and Fanny knew the barber would be back for more in a year's time, once it had grown back.

'It makes me quite sick to think of some grand lady, probably old, bald and toothless, parading about with Fanny's lovely hair tumbling down her shoulders, I can tell you!'

When I had told Joseph this story, he had just laughed and said, 'Isn't much call for your brown locks, Mary, even long as they be! Besides, the wigmaker would never get the tangles out!'

Henry, however, looked horrified.

'At least you don't laugh as Joseph did when I told him about Fanny. Tis no laughing matter to have all your hair cut off in winter. Poor Fanny was so cold without her locks and she is still made fun of to this day . . . even more than me!'

Henry looked at me sharply. 'Who is it makes fun of you, Miss Anning?'

'Oh, everybody,' I said. 'But I don't make no mind. It's water off the back of a duck to me.'

I would not show weakness. It is not my nature. I was as good as any boy or girl . . . or any man or woman, for that matter, and they should not break me with their silliness or cruel ways. Nor would I let them speak ill of my father, who taught me more than I could ever learn in school and taught me so well that I might teach this pale, rich boy who was so much older and more learned than me and yet knew so little of the real world of the poor.

'I am sorry,' he said, head bent.

'Why? It's not any fault of yours!'

'If it is of any consolation, I too am made fun of.' His face was a deep, dark red.

'You? Why should you be mocked?'

'I am mocked because of my friendship with you.'

Friendship? I had never thought of him or anyone as a friend. He was certainly useful to me, which was a good thing. I did not know whether I liked him speaking of friendship.

'Piffle. More likely it is because I am low-born or a girl or younger than you!'

'I think it is all those things and none of them.'

I was confused. How could it be all and none? I looked at him sternly, for I do not like confusion any more than I think I like friendship.

'You know how it is with bullies. They must find someone to pick on. Someone who is different in some way. Someone of whom they are secretly jealous perhaps.'

At this, I laughed. 'Who'd be jealous of *me*? If they are that foolish, they can't be at all frightening! I should not give them the time of day!'

'I'll try to be like you, Miss Anning, and ignore them.'

I was minded to discover who these fools were and teach them a lesson, but in that moment, I felt a new, strange urge which I could not ignore. I wanted to find a way to be kind to Henry.

'You can call me Mary, if you wish. Since you think we are friends.'

He smiled at me and stretched out his hand. Soft and white. I stared at it for a while and then I took it and we shook hands solemnly. Maybe it was good to have a friend. I felt warmth spread through my bones. A very curious feeling.

8
FROM MUD TO BUNS

'Will you look at that blue sky! How blissful this is, to be lying in the sun without a care in the world. After all that rain! I thought it would never stop.'

Frenchie was lying on his back on a patch of scrubby grass at the bottom of the undercliff above Monmouth Beach. He was shielding his eyes against the summer sunshine and he was right. The sky was as blue as it can be and the sea beneath sparkled and danced. He was a lazy so-and-so, some days, and I didn't mind telling him to his face.

'Some of us' – I said crossly, between gritted teeth – 'some of us have work to do. Some of us cannot be lying around staring at the sky.'

He sat up and pulled some bits of grass out of his hair. He looked sheepish. Funny term, that. Sheepish. I learned it from Mother. She said Father looked sheepish when he had been out with his friends or 'his ragtag mob of addle-pated, bottle-headed boobies' as she called them, not having much time for men who have taken too much drink.

Anyway, Henry looked more like a dog that's been caught piddling on a person and I've seen that. I really have! A fashionable lady got out of her carriage down near the Cobb, handed her dog (a pug that could lick its own eyes, its face was so flat and its tongue so long) to the footman who set it down on the ground. It looked up at him and then, bold as you like, lifted its leg and passed water all down his shiny, polished boots. He never said a thing. Just stood there, red in the face, while the dog suddenly remembered its manners and looked . . . well, looked like a dog who's just piddled on a person. Then its rich mistress gathered the dog up and made a huge fuss over it as if it had been clever. I laughed and laughed and got some very angry looks, I can tell you.

Anyway, that's how Frenchie looked.

Then he smiled. 'But you *love* what you are doing, don't you, so it's no hardship for you, is it?'

I growled and started hauling at the huge slab of earth and mud that had toppled down from the cliff top, loosened by a torrential downpour the previous night. It was nearly as big as a bed and as thick as my arm. I could see the gleam of something stuck between the layers like a flower pressed in the pages of a book. I just needed to get it on its side so I could give it a proper crack with my hammer, but it was stuck in the mud and I could not seem to get a proper grip on it. It was a moment for cursing as my father sometimes did, and I muttered some rude words under my breath which made me feel better, I must say.

'Let me do that!' Frenchie was up at last and grinning at me like a fool. 'That looks a bit big for a girlie!'

Oh! He had made me well and truly mad with fury by then, so I dug my fingers into the mud and grabbed the biggest handfuls I could. That mud is dirty stuff on a white shirt, I can tell you. Frenchie looked a bit shocked for a moment and then he was grinning again.

'Oh, Miss Anning. I mean, Mary . . . you are so easy to rile, so quick to lose your temper! I was only teasing you! I know how you hate to be called a girl!'

'You called me "girlie", which is disrespectful. A girl is as good as a boy any day! And if you know I hate it so much, why do you so do it?' I fumed, dabbling my hands in a pool to wash off the mud.

'Because you are so funny when you are cross! Your eyes blaze like a dragon's and I almost expect fire to come out of your nose!'

Hmmm. I was not offended by being likened to a dragon and I almost smiled.

I turned back to the slab. 'Come on then, you lazy creature. Help me set this upright so I can strike it fair and square.'

Henry was quite strong for all he had the soft hands of a lady and the hair of one of those cherubs in church. He watched as I brought my hammer down along the seam of rock and the whole slab split asunder as if by magic and lay in two pieces like a massive Bible opened at the centre.

We peered at the black surface. Many thousands of tiny discs like petals glinted in the sunlight.

Beautiful.

Worthless.

'Goodness me!' Henry was wide-eyed with wonder, the fool. 'What are those? They look like stars in the night sky!'

'Fish scales, you great numbskull. Nothing but fish scales. And look . . . a few fish bones.'

I was very disappointed. I'd had a strange feeling in my own bones before I struck that slab, and an even stranger feeling in my stomach, as if I had swallowed a bee and it was buzzing around my insides. But this find was not a find at all. It was worthless.

'I'm sorry, Mary.' Henry moved to touch me but I stepped back quickly out of his reach. 'I expect you thought there might be something big in there, something that would bring in plenty of money.'

Yes. I had thought that and I was disappointed, but I was more disappointed that my bones and my stomach had lied to me and had let me down. What if I had lost my magic touch? What if I never found anything valuable again?

'Don't give up, Mary,' he encouraged me. 'I'll wager you'll find a magical monster one fine day and it will make you famous and bring you fortune!'

'Pah! People like me don't make fortunes. Fortunes aren't made. They are given to rich folk by their parents. Look at you! You'll never go hungry. You'll always have a fresh laundered shirt on your back and a feather bed to sleep on. You will never have to give two seconds' thought to where your bread will come from. And as for fame! There'll be no fame for me! Who would pay me attention? A poor *girl*! I hardly count for anything on this Earth! Why, you . . . you who say you are my friend, you have never even asked me to your house! For I would bring shame upon you, wouldn't I? A poor wretch, dressed in rags. In your fine home? With your lady mother?'

I do not know why I suddenly raged about visiting his house for I had no desire to see it whatsoever, but Henry had turned red in the face from shame and that gave me some satisfaction.

'Well, you've not asked me to *your* house, either!' he retorted. 'And as for visiting us, I should think you would hate to have to wash your face and brush your hair and pretend to be nice to my mother whom you would, no doubt, judge to be an empty-headed woman and . . . and . . .'

I was wrong. It was not shame. It was anger and he wasn't done, yet.

'And you still have your father, so do not tell me how terrible your life is. I would give all the riches in the world to have my father back at home, alive, with me and my mother! You may not have much, Miss Anning, but you have so much more than me. More than you will ever know.'

With that he struck off in the direction of the town. He did not give me a backward glance. I could tell that he was wiping his eyes on his sleeves as he walked. What a strange creature! His father had been dead many months, yet he still cried for him as if it were yesterday. It was beyond my understanding. His father was dead and gone and nothing would bring him back, least of all crying. It must be very irksome to be so weak. If we had been brought low by every dead baby, we would have been fair worn out and good for nothing.

But I could not help a feeling of sadness creep over me as I watched him stumbling across the rocks, slipping on the seaweed. Maybe I could have been kinder; still, he must surely understand that I was only stating facts. Facts were facts. How could it be wrong?

'Frenchie!' I shouted as loudly as I could. 'Frenchie!'

He turned and his eyes were indeed red with crying. He just stood, staring at me. He lifted his shoulders in a shrug as if asking me what I wanted.

But then his mouth opened in a great 'O'.

He started running towards me, screaming and waving.

And then I heard it.

The rumble behind and above me. A groaning. A tearing sound.

I felt the ground beneath me start to shift as the noise grew louder and louder.

I looked up.

The cliff was on the move and heading straight for me.

Huge slabs of mud and rock and scrub were sliding from the top, gathering speed. My blood turned to ice in my veins.

'Run!' bellowed Henry. *'Run!'*

I ran as I had never run before, my chest burning, my heart pounding, trying to keep my footing on the slime of the seaweed.

I reached Henry just as the great mountain of rock and mud and stones crashed onto the beach with a thunderous boom, shaking the ground beneath our feet.

Henry threw his arms about me and near squeezed all my remaining breath clean out of my lungs. 'Thank God!' he sobbed. 'Thank *God*!'

He held me tightly for what seemed like an age and I felt

myself getting very hot and wriggly for I do not like to be held so. It made me feel wild, like a trapped animal, so I pushed him away with all my might.

What a sight he was. Red-eyed, covered in mud save for the streaks from his tears, filthy shirt (my fault, I know). He looked like any ragamuffin or ne'er-do-well. I had to laugh. So I did.

He stared at me in disbelief and then he started to laugh too. We laughed and laughed like fools. We laughed so much we had to lie down on the beach and hold our sides.

Did we think it funny or were we just glad to be still alive? I think I know.

'That was close,' Henry said, when we finally stopped our laughter.

'Pish! I've had closer escapes than that,' I said. But it was not true and I do not know why I told the lie. Maybe it was pride.

We lay there in silence for a while. I knew I owed him my gratitude but somehow I could not say the words. To be truthful, I was not pleased to be the one who needed saving. I was the one who should have been doing the saving, for the cliffs belonged to me. They were my cliffs, my domain. I suddenly felt cross and hot.

The silence was long. Then Henry sat up and stared out to sea.

'Do you want to come to tea, Mary?' he asked, wiping his face with a very muddy kerchief.

'Now you *are* making a fool out of me!' I replied, almost hoping that he wasn't.

'By no means. Come! We must celebrate!'

'Celebrate what, exactly? We did not find anything!'

'Oh, bother to that. I just saved your life even though you won't thank me for it! Come on! There may even be a sugared bun!' He stood and stretched out his hand to pull me up. 'Oh . . . and Mother is away, so we can have tea all by ourselves.'

I wished I had never said anything about visiting his house. I didn't want to go. I was afraid. I admit it. When we were on the beach, I was the ruler of my world and he was my helper. I decided when and where we went and what he had to do to help me when we got there. In his house I would be something else. I would not be the master. I did not like the feeling that came with these thoughts.

But was I not Lightning Mary? Was I not the bravest creature in Lyme, as my father said? I decided to think about the sugared bun. Surely that was reason enough to forget my fears.

I took a deep breath and leaped to my feet, brushing off the mud and sand from my skirts.

'Very well. If we must. Let's get it done.'

Henry laughed, 'Really, Mary. You are the strangest creature alive!'

'I am,' I said. 'And don't you forget it.'

How different Henry's home was from Cockmoile Square with its poky kitchen and blackened stove! There were no long johns and chemises hanging to dry from the rafters, no pan of boiling cabbage making the whole house smell as if Joseph had broken wind (which he did frequently and thought very clever).

Here there was a cook in the snowiest white apron, heaping up fresh-made buns and shaking sugar over them from a great silver pot. All was order and cleanliness and plenty. Herbs were hung to dry over the spotless range. All manner of jars and bottles and packets lined the shelves. Cherries and plums were piled up in a glass dish which sparkled in the light from the vast window. How was it possible that a short walk up Silver Street could take a body into a different world?

The cook left us to ourselves. She raised her eyebrows as far as they would go when she saw us, dirty as we were, but she said nothing. Just made the tea and set two buns from the pile on plates, smiling to herself as she did so.

I had never held such a delicate cup in my whole life. I had never tasted tea. We almost *never* had sugar in our house, but Henry added two spoonfuls of it to my cup. It was all a wonder. I burned my tongue twice but I didn't care. It tasted like the sweetness on the end of a clover flower petal (which make very good eating, I can tell you).

Once I had drunk my tea, I could not tear my eyes away from those buns. I suddenly felt as if a great monster was tearing at my belly, so hungry was I.

'Please, Mary, do help yourself!' Henry pushed the plate towards me. 'They are one of Cook's specialities.'

There was sugar all over the top of the bun. It shone like the fish scales. I wanted to lick it off but that was probably not the right thing to do. I watched as Henry bit into his and I did the same. It was the most delicious thing I had ever tasted. Then I felt a pang of guilt and, I must confess, a little fizzle of curiosity, for I have heard the stories about the sugar plantations and Henry must know the truth, since he lived where the sugar comes from and his father had a plantation. The questions piled up in my head and tumbled out almost faster than I could speak them.

'Is it true that many thousands of black people make the sugar? Is it true that rich men buy the black people at a market like sheep or cows and keep them as prisoners and never pay them? Is it true that the plants have leaves as sharp as any blade and that it cuts their hands and feet and faces? Did your father have slaves? Was he cruel to them? Did he beat them if they did not work hard?'

Henry looked away as if to ignore my questions. He set his plate down on the table and then sat on his hands as if to make himself even more uncomfortable. Or maybe to stop himself from striking me, though he is a gentle soul. He may have been angry. I couldn't tell.

'We had slaves. Yes. Yes. We did.'

'And did you treat them cruelly? Not you, I mean. Your father?'

'No. He didn't. We didn't; but it was why Father had decided to come back to England. He did not like slavery. It sickened him. It sickened him to see how some of the other plantation owners treated their workers. He was pleased when our Parliament ended the trade in slaves two years ago but that wasn't enough for him. He did not want it to be possible to own slaves. He really wanted them to be like workers here, free to work for a master or not as they chose.'

'Pah! You think we workers be free to choose? We must take work where we find it and we are meant to feel grateful!' I replied.

He smiled a strange smile. 'Yes, Mary. I know. But no one *owns* you – like owning a dog or a horse. No one has bought you and can do with you as they wish. I do not think you can imagine how that must feel. I cannot and I saw it with my own eyes. Imagine if I owned you?'

I stood up, feeling my face burning and my eyes aflame with fury! 'Nobody could *ever* own me. Ever!'

Henry laughed. 'I should think not! There isn't a leash or a harness could hold you! But just imagine I did, or my family did. I would never know if you really liked me and spoke to me because we were friends or whether you felt obliged for fear of punishment or because you were our possession.'

'Why would that matter? If I spoke to you, then I spoke to you. That's that!'

Henry seemed a bit confused by my observation. 'Yes, but it might not be genuine. What you said. We would not be true friends because we would not be equal.'

It was my turn to laugh. 'And you think we be equal now? You are a mad creature, Henry Frenchie Beach!'

'No. You are right,' he said. 'You are my superior when it comes to hunting treasure.'

'Quite right too!' said I, though I was mighty pleased that he misunderstood my meaning. 'Now, eat the remains of your bun or I will eat it for you.'

Henry did as he was told. I was satisfied.

When I got home, I didn't tell Mother or Father or Joseph where I'd been. I just put the leftover buns on the table and smiled a mysterious smile and left them standing in the kitchen with their mouths open like gawping gurnards.

9

A USEFUL FRIEND

*A*fter that, Henry often brought buns with him on our expeditions, wrapped up in a twist of paper. Sometimes I pretended not to be at all interested for I could not have him think that I was like some stray dog to be tamed with a scrap of food, but then he would sit on a rock and lick the sugar off slowly, as I had wanted to do, while laughing at me as I tried to ignore him.

'Come on, Mary. I know you are a proud one, but Cook made these for you,' he said, holding out one of the sugary temptations.

It is a hard thing to be hungry, to feel your stomach seemingly try to eat itself, but you can get used to it. You have to, or all you'd do is think about food all day, which would be of no use whatsoever.

I took the bun. He smiled. I had found out for myself how powerful it felt to be able to feed others but I did not like him to have that power over me and I did not thank him for the bun, which was very bad manners.

'I do know that I am very fortunate, Mary, and that much of my good fortune was an accident of birth.' Henry was looking at me in that 'please like me' way he had.

'Some accident,' I muttered, my mouth full of bun.

'And I know that you are proud and don't like anyone to feel sorry for you, just as you do not feel sorry for others,' he continued.

I licked my lips. 'I do feel sorry for people who suffer hardship when it is not of their own doing. There are plenty of those in Lyme. Fishermen who have lost fingers when they got caught in the nets, sailors with legs blown off by Frenchies, orphaned children,' I replied. 'I feel no such sorrow for people with more money than sense or who needlessly put their lives in danger, like those fools who go in the winter sea or try to clamber about these cliffs with no knowledge.'

'But you put yourself in danger, Mary,' said Henry. 'Must I have no sympathy for you if you are crushed in a mudslide or swept out to sea? I might not be there to save you next time!'

I smiled at his talk of saving me. Because he had done so the once, he seemed to think he would do so again, but I was able to look after myself and it was only because I had been distracted by him walking away, crying, that I had missed the signs.

'No sympathy for me, thank you!' said I. 'You may feel sorry for yourself for missing an adventure, but don't ever feel sorry for me! I know what I am doing!'

And with that I jumped up and set about cracking open a pile of rocks. Henry laughed and started to do the same, only his were all empty, as I knew they would be.

I did know what I was doing. I knew when and where to go along the coast. I could tell, mostly, which stones had curiosities in them and which did not. I was learning every day how to read the sea and her moods and I was a demon, though I say it myself, at haggling with the customers. That was something neither Joseph nor Henry could do well at all, even though they vied with each other and thought I did not notice. Joseph was stubborn about prices and made people lose patience and walk away. Henry just smiled at them and took the first offer they made, so I told him he could have no part in selling since he cost us money with his 'How-do-you-dos' and flattery and general lack of a nose for making money.

Most of the time, Joseph seemed to pretend Henry wasn't even there, but he often made remarks behind his back about his rank or clothes or abilities. Then, one day, as Henry fiddled about with the setting out of the curiosities on the stall, he spoke straight to him.

'I suppose you be too grand for trade,' he observed, and even I could hear the sneer in his voice.

'You may be right, Joseph,' Henry answered very calmly. 'I do not think I have found my métier.'

'Your whattier?' I asked, for that was a word I had never heard before.

'My métier . . . the thing I should be doing to make my way in the world. It's a French word. Sorry!'

'Ha! Always knew you were a Frenchie!' I said, but I was only teasing him and he knew it.

'Well,' said Joseph, moving everything on the table back to how it had been before Henry had rearranged it, 'there you have it. It's not your *met-ee-ay*, Frenchie.'

Henry looked like a kicked dog but he did not bite back. He just saluted me and walked away.

'That was rude,' I said.

'Well, he's of no use to us, Mary. You must see that.' Joseph's face had gone very red.

'He's of use to me!' I retorted. 'He is company on my excursions and carries my finds.' I nearly added that he brought me buns but decided that was best kept quiet as it would be another reason to make Joseph cross.

'Well, how very pleasant for him that he does not have to

79

work for a living. Unlike some of us. Used to be just me and you, Mary, thick as thieves. Now I am nothing but a pig in the middle.'

So, it was jealousy.

'There is nothing to stop you coming out with us of an evening!' I said.

'When I am weary from a day's labour?' he replied.

There is no pleasing some people.

Mother had a saying: 'No good deed goes unpunished'. She was right. The next three evenings, Joseph came too, and we got less work done than if it were just me on my own, for the boys argued and bickered and tried to outdo each other with the size of rock they'd attempt to move or the steepness of the cliff they'd try to climb.

I found all this very dull and annoying for they were very noisy at the same time, squawking away like gulls fighting over a bit of bread. Why do boys have to show off as if they are cockerels in a hen house? Tis easy to see why there be so many wars, with them so anxious to scrap with their own kind it's hardly surprising that they rush to pick fights with folk who are different.

Why, even I have been learned to be afear'd of the French with all the tales of what they do to prisoners and how they eat all manner of disgusting things like frogs' legs and snails.

But then I got to thinking that they might be very poor and starving, even. Or maybe they just like eating them. After all, we eat whelks and cockles and what are they but snails of the sea? I couldn't eat a frog's leg, however hungry I felt. I was certain of that.

All the same, I prayed that Henry and Joseph were not called away to fight at sea, however much they seemed keen to fight on land, Joseph being the worse of the two for getting his fists out. When Joseph heard someone say that there were press gangs up the coast in Weymouth looking for poor souls to go and fight Napoleon, Mother forbade him to go out of the house for fear he'd be snatched and taken off for a Navy man. She knew that if they got him, they'd return him broken and useless or, worse, she'd never see him again alive. It was no adventure for a common sailor. No doubt it was different for the officers in all their finery and with all the money they made from the spoils of war. Anyway, Joseph was safe for the press gangs never came to Lyme and for that I was very glad.

I must admit that I was mightily relieved when Joseph tired of our company and decided to go fishing in the evenings instead. Peace and quiet returned.

I have always liked it to be quiet. Sometimes, when I am very intent on winkling out some curio or ferreting about in the mud for signs of something worth digging out, I find even the slap of the waves on the shore irritating. Inside my head there is so much questioning and enquiring. It's as if I have got lots of extra Mary Annings running about in my brain, thinking and spying and wondering and trying to work things out and if any other sounds get in, it sends all those Marys quite mad. It sounds strange, I know, but that is how it is and just one tiny squeak can be too much when I am concentrating.

Sometimes, I concentrated so hard that I was in another world entirely and time passed without me even noticing. I forgot everything. I forgot to be hungry or thirsty (which is good as there was nothing to eat or drink unless Henry brought it) and I forgot about having a piss, so that when I got home I had to rush to find the chamber pot because I was bursting fuller than the biggest flagon you could ever imagine. I know that is not ladylike, but I am trying to explain how it was for me and besides, I am no lady, as well you know by now.

That was one good thing about Henry. He learned my funny ways and he changed his ways to suit mine. He would like to hum while he made his drawings but that was something I couldn't abide. When first he did it, bumbling away like a bee on a buttercup, I looked at him with the most foul face I could muster. Then I threw mud at him and then I went and thumped him soundly and that stopped him. After that, I had only to look at him with what he called 'the evil eye' and he would stop his buzzing instantly, and after a while he never did it any more, so long as we were alone. When Joseph was there too, all my rules were disregarded and it fair made my head boil so that I was driven to move as far away from them as I could.

So, as long as I could keep Joseph and Henry apart that long summer, I preferred Henry to be with me. For the fact was, Henry really was very useful. He could draw a thing so that it almost looked real. He took out a measure and wrote down exactly how big the item was and made sure his drawing matched that faithfully. He said it was 'scientific' (a word I pretended not to hear) and that we must keep a proper record of all that we had found and where we had found it.

It was very useful when he made a drawing of a particular spot on the cliff so that we could find it again if we needed to when we returned. Usually I remembered exactly where I had left something interesting but, of course, the sea, the wind and the rain could rearrange things so that all looked different, even in the summer. Unless there had been a terrible storm or a big landslip, the top of the cliff stayed constant, so Henry looked for a landmark, like a tree or an odd-shaped bush or rock and sketched it and wrote little notes like *three paces along from this*. And that's where he would mark down an arrow pointing to the drawing of the crooked tree or the rock that looked like a face or whatever thing had caught his eye as a clue.

He was teaching me to draw too, and to label things. It pleased me to see his drawings, so plain and so clear. He called them sketches but I called mine scratches because the pen nib made a scratching noise as I wrote and caught on the paper, near enough ripping it like a cat's claw. I wished I could write as fair as he did, but I had not had the learning nor the practice so I had to do the best I could and try to get better.

When we had had a good day, there was nothing that pleased me more than when we sat down to go through all we had found and sort them into their kind and make a record of their number and size.

'What do you think these really are?' Henry asked me one day as we stood in the shallows, washing the mud off the curios. I looked at the objects he had in his hand.

'Devil's toenails and Devil's fingers of course! You know that!' I wondered at him asking such a question after all this time. He must have made drawings of twenty or thirty, maybe more.

'But they aren't, are they? Devil's toenails and fingers. I mean, how many toes does the Devil have, if any? Doesn't the Devil have a cloven hoof, like a goat? So what *are* they? Have you ever seen creatures like this alive?'

'I *know* they aren't toenails . . . but they do have a look of a toenail and the fancy folk do love to think they have the Devil's toe clippings in their hands. You must have marked how the ladies scream and wrinkle up their noses! They find delight in being disgusted, seems to me! And the fingers, dark as they be, are more like to be the finger of a devil than a lady.'

'Yes, I know,' said Henry. 'But we need to be more scientific! What *are* they? The toenails look to me like oysters or mussels but they are not the same as either. They resemble them but no more. Have you ever seen an oyster like this in all your days in Lyme? No! And neither have I! This is some ancient creature, dead for years and years!'

'We'd get no money for an old oyster. You do understand how trade works by now, don't you?' I asked.

'I do, but I also understand that you have a strong liking for truth, Mary, and I should think you would want to know what a thing really was and not to sell it as something it is not. And these' – he held up more of the Devil's toenails – 'are not toenails and these' – he pointed to the sorted heaps on the ground – 'are not serpents or ladies' fingers *or* crocodile teeth, are they? So what are they? And where are they now? The living ones, I mean.'

These were questions I had asked myself so many times and I felt pleased and cross that Henry was asking them too; pleased because we thought alike, but cross because I had never spoken of these mysteries before and Henry might think I was copying him.

He stared at me intently, awaiting my answer, but I did

not know what to say for my head went suddenly empty and then very full again with all sorts of ideas and notions, none of which I could get hold of for long enough to give it words.

He sighed. 'You are right, though. People want to believe what they want to believe; but we, Mary, *we* are going to be scientists and we will make studies and work out just what these things really are and what they mean about all of this!' He swung around, pointing at the sea, the sky and the cliff. 'What they mean about life and this Earth.'

Scientists! A word not to be said out loud. A word and a notion as bad as any talk of the Devil and yet, alongside the shiver of fear at its mention, I felt a flicker of a flame leap in my chest and there was a moment of white light in my head, as if the lightning was striking me a second time. Henry must have seen something in my face, for he smiled.

'Aha! I see you understand me, Mary. Here. Let's make a pact. Let us promise that we will be scientists – secret scientists, if you prefer – and solve these mysteries together! You have a genius for finding the evidence, while I have a modest talent for recording it. Together, our two brains can fathom out what all of this means. Do I have your promise?'

He stretched out his hand (not so white as once it was) and I shook it. I felt his determination in that firm grip and I squeezed his hand back hard as I could to show him mine. Scientists! We were to be secret scientists!

10
FRIENDSHIP LOST

*O*nly a week later and my good spirits were destroyed.

We had just finished our first day of being scientists since our pact. Autumn had brought winds and rain which kept us off the cliff for days and the mud was such that our finds were few, even with my genius for discovery. We were going back nearly empty-handed and I was not best pleased.

Henry was running to keep up as I walked off homeward at my usual brisk pace.

'Wait, Mary. There is something I must say. I want to thank you. I have had so much enjoyment and learned so much in the past few months and you've helped me to forget my grief. I am eternally grateful. More than you can ever know.'

'Well, I am glad of that,' I replied. 'For grief is a sorry waste of time in my opinion. It does not bring back the dead nor does it entertain the living.'

He smiled a little at this for, even after so much time has passed, he still could not entirely accept my plain talk.

'I want you to have this.' He handed me the little leather-bound book of his sketches, and I leafed through the drawings: a fine record of our many hours of treasure-hunting.

'Why are you giving me this?' I asked. 'There are still pages to fill and our studies have scarce begun!'

He looked downcast. 'I have been keeping something from you, Mary. I did not want to spoil everything. But the day has arrived. My time here is at an end. I am to go to the Royal Military College in Great Marlow in January and Mother and I are returning to London to visit relatives and make preparations before I go. I must be fitted out with all manner of uniforms and accoutrements! I shall be quite the popinjay!'

'But you are only a boy!' For in truth, he looked a deal younger than Joseph even though he was two years older. Maybe it was his golden curls that made him appear like a child.

'Joseph has been apprenticed and working for months. What is my excuse? I will be fourteen in a few months and the time has come. Besides, we are at war, Mary. I must do my duty.'

'But you are to be a scientist! We are to be scientists! You cannot go to be a soldier! You promised! We made a pact! You promised!'

He looked away. Crying again, I supposed. 'It's not my choice. It is what is expected. Demanded. I am sorry. It was as big a shock to me as it is to you now. Even though it was always the plan. Life cannot be so carefree for ever. You know that better than most.'

I felt a terrible feeling go through me. I did not know what it was and I still do not. I felt as if I could be sick or faint or scream or shout or do something . . . something violent. Before I knew it, I had thumped him hard on the chest and sent him reeling, coughing and gasping.

'Well, go, then. I shall be glad to be rid of you, for you are nothing but an encumbrance' – this is a very good big word I have learned from my mother – 'and a burden. Take your stupid scribblings too, for I've no need of them.'

I threw his book at him. He did not catch it, but just let it fall into the mud, where he gazed on it sorrowfully.

'I will miss you, Mary. You have been a friend to me. I will never forget you. Ever. Mark my words, you will be a famous scientist one day. A celebrated geologist. You'll solve the mystery of life on Earth and how these creatures came to be entombed in rock. You'll find monsters, treasures beyond anything we have uncovered so far. Of that, I am sure. Please, Mary! Will you not shake hands? I want us to part as friends. Please.'

There was entreaty in his voice. I am not in the habit of

being swayed by emotion, but I was gripped by such a storm of feelings myself that I barely knew what I was doing. I stuck out my hand, muddy and covered in scratches, nails black with Blue Lias clay and then snatched it away again.

'You said we would be scientists together. You *promised*! A week ago! Just one week ago! You are a liar!'

I threw the few finds we had made to the ground where they joined his sketchbook. Then I gathered up my skirts and turned to run.

I could hear him shouting to me. Something about writing to me. I did not look behind me once and his words were lost on the wind and the rushing in my ears.

I ran as fast as I could, sometimes stumbling on the cliff path, sometimes slipping on the mud, and as I ran I felt a great hatred for the cliffs and for Henry and for all that wasted time making my first friend, only to lose him.

My mother tried to stop me as I tore through the kitchen but I would not be stopped. I threw myself on the bed and screamed into the blanket. I screamed and screamed and screamed and I did not know why I felt so much pain. I had no wound. I had no broken bones. I had pain, pain that made me scream so that I did not know how to stop.

But I did stop at last. I had screamed enough for a lifetime. I could scream no more. I slept. Wild dreams filled my head. Henry and me, buried beneath that landslip. Henry sucked out to sea, shouting to me. Me, sinking in mud, fighting to break free.

The next day, I went to Black Ven and found his sketchbook where it lay in the mud, a little dampened by the dew, surrounded by the scattered treasures. I hid the book in a hole in the graveyard wall where I had first met Henry De la Beche. Frenchie.

I already missed him.

11

THE TREACHERY OF
BLACK VEN

*F*or a while, I lost the will to go treasure-hunting. With Henry gone and Father busy making a dining table and chairs for Squire Stock and his wife, I stopped going out on the seashore. I flipped and flopped about the house until Mother despaired and sent me on an errand to see if Harry May, Father's fisherman friend, had a few mackerel to spare.

I found him on the Cobb, cleaver raised to strike the head from an eel. As the blade fell, the beast wriggled and twisted and, leaving its head gushing blood, escaped Harry's grip and tumbled back into the harbour. It was like it was alive, only it was stone dead. Or so Harry said. Stone dead at the bottom of the sea, in the mud, while its head with all its monstrous teeth sat oozing on the wall, all mouth and no monster. Harry was mighty cross with himself, I can tell you, and swore like one of the rough sailors who fall out of the alehouses pretty much the same way as the eel fell off the Cobb wall. Some of *them* drown too.

'That conger would have been supper for a fair few,' Harry said sadly. He had promised me a bit if I liked, as he swung the cleaver. I did not like, as it happens, for it looked like a serpent to me and it was as slimy as a bucket of slugs. I was not sorry to see it tumble into the water.

But I could not take my eyes off the head.

'Could I have it?' I asked Harry.

He looked at me as if I was mad! 'Have what? The head?'

'Yes. Please.'

I do not know why I wanted it but I had that feeling in my bones. That same feeling that lets me know when there is a treasure in a rock. Perhaps I was feeling like a scientist, even without Henry with me.

'Well, you are a strange child to be sure, but I never took you for a bloodthirsty type! Still, you can have it once the missus has boiled the meat off for a broth. Might be a few days afore it's ready and it'll be only the skellington, mind!'

He meant the skull, but I did not correct him. The skull was all I wanted. I did not want the blackish greenish hide or the coating of grey slime, or the thick red cord of blood that ran through the skull or the great dead eyes. I just wanted to see how that head worked, with its huge jaws and teeth.

I nodded my yes and went home, ideas buzzing in my

head. I had seen plenty of fish bones and found the skulls of sheep and cows in the grass beyond the graveyard. These were strange enough compared with the live beasts. I thought a sheep had a small mouth. If you watch it eating, it just twists its nose to and fro like a baby on the breast or Mother chewing a piece of bread with her mouth tight-closed (not like Joseph who eats with his mouth open so you can see the bread tossed around like a knot of seaweed in the waves). When you see the skull, the teeth go near up to its great eye hole. Sometimes you just find the bottom bit, fallen away from the skull. The teeth are all flat like the stone for milling flour at the Town Mill. If I feel my jaw when I am chewing, I can feel it right up to my ear and it must be on a hinge like the lid of a box. How are the two parts attached? Why do they come apart in death?

I knew I would understand more when I saw the eel's bones. I wondered how many teeth it had and how wide it could open its mouth.

When I got home, Mother was sitting in a chair, mending one of Father's shirts. She smiled at me and moved to make a space for me to sit next to her.

I knew what this meant. Mother meant to talk to me about stuff I hate. I stood next to her but ignored her as she patted the chair.

'Come on, my big girl! I've got some news for you!' she

said and she tried to pull me close. I wriggled free and watched her to see what she would do next.

'Oh, Mary! A little brother or sister will join us in the spring. A blessing from God!' she said, patting her stomach.

So that was her news. Some creature was growing. Yet another mouth to feed.

I must have pulled a face, because she continued: 'You'll have babies of your own one day, Mary, and then you will understand.'

I ignored this. Babies are such a waste of time and money. I had no time for them nor never would. I determined to speak only of things which interested me.

'I saw an eel have its head chopped off today . . . a conger eel . . . and it escaped into the sea . . . just the body . . . and I am going to have the skull. Harry said I could.'

Mother sighed and shook her head. 'Oh, Mary. Whatever did that lightning do to that poor head of yours? You are a strange creature indeed.'

I smiled. I like to be strange. Ordinary is what most people are and I am not. I am not ordinary at all. I am a secret scientist.

That week the weather turned bad. October storms, the like of which had not been seen for many years, lashed the shores. The sea was grey, black, green and black again by turns. It roared and howled and smashed itself against the Cobb. The rain lashed down. The river Lym burst its banks again and thundered down Coombe Street and out to sea.

Father forbade me to go treasure-hunting with or without him. 'Especially now you are on your own!' he said, winking at me. 'Yes, my little lightning streak! Don't you think that I don't know about your accomplice! Still, he's gone and now it is too dangerous for you to be out there. Far too dangerous. Your mother would never forgive me if I let you go, so be a good girl and make yourself useful sorting these findings for me. I'll maybe teach you to use my chisels and then you can clean them up properly.'

He gave me a great pail of rock he had collected that morning after one of the most furious storms.

'Here. I cannot let you go to the cliff but here is a bit of the cliff come to you. See what you can make of this and I'll bring you more this evening! The storms have been good to us! There are riches aplenty!'

That meant that the land had moved a great deal and would be as treacherous as it could be.

Father caught my eye. 'No, Mary. Do not look to change my mind. You cannot come with me. You must stay here. I have promised your mother and I cannot go back on my word. There's a good girl.'

'Can I go to Harry and get my eel skull?' I asked. 'He might think I don't want it any more.'

'Tomorrow. If you go today, your mother will think you're with me and no amount of telling her will persuade her otherwise.'

'But doesn't she know where you are going anyway?' I retorted.

'She don't! And don't you go telling her, there's my little flash of lightning! She'll boil me alive!'

He ruffled my hair, picked up his sack and went off up towards the church and the cliff path.

I should have told him to be careful, to stay safe, but I did not and thought nothing of it at that moment.

I fetched my hammer, filled another pail with water and sat down on the doorstep. I started to pick my way through the lumps and clumps of mud and stone. I made three piles. One to my left – items I felt sure would turn out to be nothing. One to my right: hidden treasures, for sure. One in front of me; they might be treasures or they might be nothing. I tackled them first.

I washed off the mud and gave each a blow with my hammer. Three crocodile teeth and one of the Devil's fingers. He must have many hands or very many fingers because Henry and I have found more than one hundred and so that is a scientific reason why I know they are something else entirely. Some people foolishly call them thunderbolts but I am an expert in thunderbolts and I can tell you that they are too small. I also found a scuttle, just like my very first find. I wasn't excited this time.

There was nothing of much value in that pile but I washed it all off and set it aside.

I considered for a long time which pile to do next. Which would bring more satisfaction? To find treasures where I thought there would be none or to find nothing where I thought to find something special? Both were bad. Both meant that the feeling in my bones could not be trusted. I felt a little fizzle of fear and then everything suddenly went very dark as a black cloud took over the sky.

I felt strange. Mother sometimes shuddered and said a goose had walked on her grave, which was a very silly thing to say as she was not in her grave and why should it matter if a goose walked over it if she was, anyway? That moment, though, I felt very strange and thought immediately of that goose. It came into my head as clearly as if it stood before me and it looked straight at me with its yellow eyes before it vanished.

The rain started. The Devil's fingers glistened. They looked as if they might creep away. I quickly gathered them up in my skirt and went inside.

Mother was standing at the table as if frozen to the spot.

'Mother?' I said, for she was staring straight ahead, looking right through me.

'Mary!' She seemed to see me at last. 'A goose just walked over my grave!'

I do not believe in ghoulies and ghosties or people who say they can see the future or anything stupid like that, but it gave me a fright to hear her say that. It gave me a fright and made me feel sick too.

Mother must have seen my face change at her words for she rushed towards me and nearly smothered me in a hug which is, as you know, not something I enjoy. This time, though, I did not struggle free but let her hold me, even though my face was squashed against her so that I could barely breathe and my hands, holding the treasures in my skirts, were pinned tight to me. She smelled of onions and a rather nasty cheesy smell very like Joseph's stockings so I just didn't sniff again and, after a minute or two, she let me go. I lost my balance and dropped the Devil's fingers and the scuttle on the floor. But before I could pick them up, she took hold of my shoulders, the better to stare into my eyes.

'Where is your father, Mary?' she demanded.

'Will you boil him alive if I tell you?' I asked. I was trying so hard to please them both, you see.

Her eyes narrowed as she let go of me. 'He's on that blasted beach, isn't he? He's on that blasted beach fossicking about with nary a care in the world for us as must bide here and wait for him, afear'd for him. That man! I could murder him!'

I nearly said that he was safer on the cliffs if she wanted to murder him there in the kitchen but I held my tongue.

She tore off her apron and flung it to the ground so hard that a cloud of dust blew up and then she kicked the curiosities across the room. I watched them closely to see where they ended up. With luck they would not be chipped or broken.

Then she started to sob. She shook. Her shoulders went up and down with each great cry. Finally she turned to me again. Her face was blotchy; her eyes had all but disappeared. 'I have a bad feeling, Mary. A bad feeling. And you do too. I saw it in your face.'

'Bad feelings cannot make bad things happen!' I said.

'Maybe not. But what if the bad thing has already happened? What then?'

'Well, if it has happened, it has happened and there's nothing to be done about it,' said I. But these were brave words which hid my fears. I calmed myself by fixing my eyes on the treasures but I didn't pick them up. 'Besides, you said you could murder him, which would be a very bad thing indeed.'

She growled with annoyance. 'As if I meant that. You do deliberately misunderstand a body, Mary.'

But I was not really listening and she caught me staring at the scuttle wedged under the dresser.

Her face reddened with anger. 'Get those blasted things out of my sight!'

I gathered them and took them upstairs to hide under the blanket on my side of the bed and then went back down to wait.

Mother had calmed down quite a bit. Leastways, she had stopped crying. She was preparing a stew of potatoes and the last of the leeks, but she was distracted. I could see that she'd cut a finger off if she did not give the knife more of her attention. That'd be all the meat there'd be in that stew. I thought of asking if I could go and find Harry and see if his wife Christa had boiled my eel skull clean yet, but thought I had better stay and watch over Mother after all.

I still felt sick. For all my brave talk and not believing silly stories about geese and graves, I knew in my bones that something bad had happened, but I wouldn't give in and cry. I just sat tight and thought about the eel skull.

Henry suddenly came into my mind, pushing the eel out. I recalled his words: *'I hope, for your sake, that you never have to lose your father.'* I'd scoffed at him. Of course Father would die one day. Everything living dies one day . . . or night.

Just not tonight.

Please.

It was as black as pitch by the time Joseph came home from his labours. He went straight back out again to see if Father was in his workshop but I knew he would not find him there.

I was thinking terrible thoughts. I could not stop myself.

Father buried in mud, his eyes and ears and nose and mouth full of the black ooze. Not able to see. Not able to breathe. Not able to scream.

Or Father snatched by the sea and swallowed up.

Or snatched by the sea and then thrown back against the rocks, smashed like a toy.

Try as I might, I could not drive these images from my mind.

Then my waking nightmares were broken by a knock at the door.

Two men. Only one I recognised: Harry, the strong white-haired beheader of eels, his face as tanned as a bit of leather. I've always liked his twinkly blue eyes but they were not twinkly that night. He looked pale and anxious. He had not come to give me my eel skull, that was certain.

'Hello, little Mary. Is Molly there?'

I could feel Mother suddenly behind me. She laid her hands on my shoulders for the second time that day and pulled me close again. I held my breath.

'Is it Richard, Harry? Is he . . . ? Is he . . . ?'

She couldn't say the word, the terrible word which would end all hope of happiness at a stroke.

'No. Not . . .' Seemed Harry could not say it, either. And I was more glad than I could say that he had no need to. But there was a 'but' – I could hear it in his voice.

'There's been an accident. Seems Richard was up on the top path on Black Ven. He must have thought to take a short cut home. Anyways, the long and the short of it, is that he fell. He fell a long way, Molly. There's men out there now carrying him back. You need to be ready for what you will see, you and your children, for he is not a well man. Not . . . dead, praise be, but not well neither.'

My mother gripped my shoulders so tightly that I could feel a scream rising in my throat. I bit my lip to stop from crying out. I despised crying. I would not cry. Not again.

I could see some shapes emerging from the dark beyond Harry. Four men held the corners of a canvas sail which sagged from the weight of the man it carried.

Father!

They brought him into the house and set him on the table. The lantern's pale light showed him to be near enough covered top to toe in mud but, running in little rivers from his head and down his cheek, was the bright, bright red of his life's blood.

Mother took hold of the nearest thing to hand to clean his

face. It was my pinny for Sunday School, but I did not mind. She stroked his face with a tenderness I had not marked before.

'That's a girt big gash on his forehead, Molly,' said one of the men. 'He's knocked himself senseless, seemingly.'

'Senseless,' sighed my mother. 'He was senseless the day he got it into his head to walk on Black Ven. A treacherous place if ever there was one. I warned him, and nobody can say I did not. I told him t'would be the death of him one day or of the children. But he wouldn't listen. Always a headstrong man. Well, he's paid for it now and that's a fact. I always said, there's nothing but dead creatures as comes off Black Ven and here he is, near enough a dead creature himself.'

She had bathed away the mud and now I could see the deep cut beneath the matted hair.

'Must it be sewn up, Mother?' asked Joseph, who had come to join us at the table.

'No money for surgeons, Joe,' said my mother sadly. 'He shall have to do with Nurse Molly.' She turned to the men. 'I thank you, friends and neighbours, for bringing him back. You had better leave me to clean him as best I can. Joe will call you back to help us get him to his bed.'

'We'll wait in the alehouse,' said Harry and, catching her eye, 'but only so as to be close. We'll not let a drop pass our lips afore we get Richard to his bed.'

I stroked my father's poor head, willing him with all my might to open his eyes just like he had willed me to do when the lightning struck me. 'Come on, Father! Open your eyes for your Mary!'

For one moment, his lids fluttered like a butterfly's wings, and then he slept again.

12

A STRUGGLE BETWEEN
LIFE AND DEATH

*H*enry told me that his father was alive one day and dead the next. He said he wished he had known he was going to die so that he could say goodbye to him before he went.

Father seemed like to die for weeks, but he didn't, not even when he seemed almost gone, when his eyes were open but he seemed to be seeing nothing, when he ate nothing, said nothing, did not move. Mother would lift his head and tip a little water in between his lips and he would swallow some but let most of it run out of his mouth and down his beard.

I thought about Henry and his father, taken from him with no warning. Was this my chance to say goodbye? It seemed to me that if I said goodbye, I should be excusing him and letting him go when we needed him to get better. So I did not say it. I held his hand, mopped his brow, showed him my finds and talked to him as if he was listening. I had even thought to share a letter from Henry with him, but none came.

Joseph and I shared Mother and Father's bed so that we might all help to keep Father warm. Winter was upon us and nights were long and cold. Days were scarce different – short and cold. We were all exhausted but we got little sleep. Father moaned and cried out and passed water in the bed for he could not rise to use the pot, so we lay there awake, feeling the hot wetness of his piss turn cold beneath our bodies and listening to his wails and Mother's sobs.

I was sickened to see him brought so low. He was once so strong. He could swing me up onto his shoulders with no effort at all. He could heave half a tree trunk onto a cart by himself. He could move a slab of mud and rock on the beach as easily as if it were a pebble. Now he could not lift his own head, with its mess of dirty, greying hair, all tangled and stiff with sweat and tears, and his arms were thin and wasted, the skin yellowed and slack. You could near enough count every bone in his hands and feet and sometimes I tried, tracing their whiteness beneath the skin.

I thought he might wake up enough to pay attention to the eel's skull. Harry had tied the two parts of the skull together with a piece of string and I amused myself making the jaws snap together as if the eel were still alive. The teeth! Front ones long and sharp and curved towards its throat. I put one hand into its maw and pretended to be a fish, trying to wriggle free. Once behind those teeth, there was no escape, I could see – and feel. I had little cuts on my knuckles to prove their sharpness. Behind these daggers, a row of needles for chewing the flesh to a pulp ran all the way to the back of its throat, beyond the great holes where its eyes had been. I ran my finger over them and drew blood again.

I sat by Father, snapping and unsnapping those jaws, imagining if the eel were twice the size, three times the size. What a monster it would be! A dragon, fierce as any fought by St George!

I wished Henry was there with me. I would like to have shown him that eel. He could have made a drawing of it for me. I could have talked to him about Father. Maybe he would have known what to do for the best.

I would not have told him everything. I wouldn't have told him about the pissing in the bed or the way Father dribbled or that he was getting very thin and nearly see-through or that he smelled disgusting, even though Mother washed him down on the days that were not freezing, and I was sure that he would not have asked about all that, but he would have helped me to believe that Father would get well again. I was sure of that. Perhaps, though, the plain truth was that I would never hear from him again. 'Out of sight, out of mind' went the saying. No doubt it was true.

The good news was that the people of Lyme Regis were, for the most part, kinder than they'd ever been when Father was well. We discovered who our true friends were. Some righteous folk helped out of a wish to turn us all from chapel back to church, going on about their Christian duty and making it very plain that they helped for no other reason. It was very hard to take their coin or bread when they felt obliged to add that 'he brought it on himself' and that 'God punishes the wicked', meaning we Dissenters, and that we were 'the poor innocents suffering as a consequence of Father's wilfulness'. Joseph ordered me to bite my lip and hold my tongue and I did, though my face told the truth . . . or so the horrid woman from St Michael's said as she thrust a wizened turnip and two carrots in my hands.

'I seen him!' she crowed, her evil eyes sparkling like chips of quartz in a rock. 'Up on Black Ven on the Sabbath! Dragging you poor souls with him and away from the Lord! Let this be a warning to him. He has been spared to show God's mercy and that he might return to the one true church! The Lord be praised!'

Joseph stood by me and pinched my back as I took her miserable leavings. I wanted to say something. I wanted to say that I did not believe she would find herself in Heaven when her time came and that I could not help but hope that time would be soon, carrots or no. But I was good and stayed silent. She saw the black look of hatred which Joseph said passed over my face like a storm cloud over the sea and shook her bony finger at me. 'I see that ingratitude, child. I see the Devil in your face. You are your father's daughter and no mistake! Unnatural!'

I did not care. Let her see what was in my heart! I wanted to kick her down the steps.

'She means well,' said Joseph when she'd gone.

Hmmm. Indeed. I'd have liked to see her mean ill, then!

Mother had a strong dislike of charity for she was proud like me, but the baskets of food had been a blessing, she said, and, truth to tell, we were better fed some days than we ever were before, which was good for the unborn as well as the living. I don't think she still believed the baby that grew in her belly was a blessing but it was, at least, another reason why Father must get well.

Harry May brought us a bit of salt fish two or three days every week for a month and that was most kind of him, for the weather did not allow sea fishing and he was sharing what must have been the last of his supplies, set aside for the winter. Even when winter was nearly done, spring storms could keep the boats ashore as much as any snow or ice. Folk had to survive on what they had kept from harvest – salted, pickled, preserved somehow.

Squire Stock, one of Father's customers, sent us eggs,

milk and cheese from time to time. At least the cold meant that the milk stayed fresh for many days, instead of curdling and going sour as it did in summer. Mother warmed a little for Father and tried not to mind when it spilled down his nightshirt. On good days, she managed to get him to swallow a morsel of coddled egg. He ate so little, grew so thin, but still he didn't die.

When I wasn't sitting with Father and Joseph was not at his apprenticeship, we carried on doing our best to make sure there were plenty of treasures to sell when the visitors arrived.

Joe and I were never much given to squabbles (except where Henry was concerned), but I knew it irked him that treasures seemed to leap out of the mud and into my hands whilst he dug and scraped for leaner pickings. It pleased me, of course. I cannot pretend it does not still, but I have never crowed or boasted about it. Even to this day, Joe complains sometimes that it wasn't fair and I know he thought it wasn't fair because I was younger than him *and* a girl! Mainly because I was a girl. Why that should have made any difference, I have never really understood. I suppose many would think it strange if Joseph could sew a frock or dress a baby, but why one thing should be for a boy to do and another only for a girl was beyond my understanding. It was quite ridiculous. I could thump any boy pretty much as hard as he could thump me, if I'd a mind to, as Henry found to his cost, but it wasn't just about thumping. It was everything. Girls were just expected to stay at home and cook and clean for men, far as I could see. And have babies or lose them.

That baby of Mother's, planted before the accident, gave up living before it was ready to be born. I found Mother one day, huddled in the corner of the bedchamber, clutching a little bundle of bloodstained rags and moaning to herself. I had seen this before but this time it seemed both cruel and a blessing at the same time. Mother had suffered enough. She loved babies. I did not. I was glad that there would be no crying babe, taking all her attention and laying her low, and I could not understand why they mattered to her so much but they did and that was that. She had had nothing but hardship these past months and I did not wish her any more.

'Must we have a burial, again?' I asked, as gently as I could. But she shook her head.

'No, child. It was scarce there. Scarce formed. A scrap, poor mite.'

I did not ask her why she cried so hard for a scrap. I left her to her grief, and when the time came for bed there was no trace of blood or rags or the baby that never really was. I do not think Father even knew that it had been and gone so fast. It was a loss to her alone.

Having lost yet one more infant and with a husband ailing

and still like to die, Mother was not best pleased about us going back onto the eastern beaches below Black Ven or Monmouth's western shores. However, when we returned one day with thirty snakestones and the largest, most sparkling lump of what we called angel's wings, we could see her doing sums in her head and reckoning the money that could be unlocked by selling those finds.

I took the angel's wings up the stairs to show Father. The golden rock was as large as my two fists. It looked so curious, as if a mass of wood chips and shards of broken glass and nail heads and buttons had all been melted together and turned into gold. When I looked at it closely, I could see that it resembled coal too. Gold coal. What strange matter! If I were a true scientist, I would know exactly what it was.

I was going to lay it on Father's chest, as if it were a gift, but it was so heavy that it might have crushed him, for his bones were like a bird's. Instead, I drew back the curtain so that the sunlight struck it and sent beams of golden light around the room.

'Father! Look! It is an angel, come to visit!'

He opened his eyes and then closed them again as a shaft of light dazzled him. I moved away from the window.

He opened his eyes again. He smiled. A very small smile.

I had not seen Father smile for what seemed like for ever.

He moved his lips to speak but they were cracked and dry

so I set down my prize and gave him a sip of water. He swallowed it all without dribbling. He tried to sit up but he was too weak.

'Mary!' So faint, I could scarcely hear.

I climbed on the bed and put my ear near his lips.

'My little Lightning Mary!' he whispered and he lifted his scrawny arm and held out his hand. I rested my hand in his. It felt like a bundle of twigs. The palm was cool and damp. I did not like the touch of it but I was pleased to feel those twiggy fingers close around my own.

'You aren't going to die, after all!' I said. 'I thought you were, but you were taking a long time over it so I thought maybe you would get well after all. That is what I told Mother but she has been worrying so and it's been horrible for us and did you know you piss the bed and dribble and groan all night long so we can get no sleep and you weren't even interested in my eel skull and—'

He gave my hand a feeble squeeze. 'Hush! Hush!' he whispered.

He closed his eyes and for one moment I wondered if I that had been my chance to say goodbye and instead I had talked nothing but nonsense.

But then he opened his eyes and smiled again. 'Oh, Mary! May you never change!'

'I never will!' I said.

'That's my girl.'

He closed his eyes and let go of my hand. I wiped it on my skirt because it was all clammy from his touch.

'Do you want to see my eel skull now?' I asked, but he shook his head very slightly.

'Tired. Tomorrow.' And with that he fell back to sleep.

I went down to tell Mother.

'He's talking. He wants to see my eel skull tomorrow. We must give him an egg tonight to build up his strength.'

'Must we, indeed,' said Mother. 'There are but two remaining and I had thought to give them to you and Joseph, now you are both shooting up like bean poles.'

'Father needs it more than me. Besides, I don't want to grow more. My clothes are too tight as it is. I can scarce breathe and you can nearly see my knees in this dress.' It was true that my few clothes were becoming very tight and I did not like the feel of them at all.

Mother looked at me long and hard. I thought she might be about to cry. 'You're becoming a woman, Mary! You'll be all growed up soon. With babbies of your own and a man by your side to look after you.'

At that moment, Joseph came in and it was just as well for I think I would have screamed with fury. Mother knows I do not like talk of babies or husbands.

'Mary'll never be wed!' said Joseph. 'She can't abide

anyone in her company except we three and that fancy boy of hers.'

My face grew hot with anger, but I bit my tongue and said nothing for, in truth, I did not know what to say. I had been riled by his rude description of Henry but I was also befuddled for a moment by a strange feeling that I might cry.

'Don't tease her, Joe, there's a good lad. She will come around to a husband and babies soon enough.'

'I will not,' I muttered under my breath, my hands balled in tight fists ready to thump Joseph or Mother if they continued in this vein. 'I will never, ever. I will not be a man's skivvy. I will not let myself grow fat with child or spend my days cleaning and cooking and waiting on a man like a slave with no life but what some, some *man*, says I must have!' I spat out the words and a big gobbet of spittle landed on the floor. Joseph saw and started to laugh which enraged me. 'Some stupid man, like you are becoming, Joseph Anning!' and I pushed past him to go outside.

'Wait here, missy!' shouted Mother. 'That's no way to speak to me or your brother!'

I stopped and turned round. 'Why? Because you be so superior? Because you be so *old*?'

'Mary, Mary!' sighed Mother. 'We have had difficult times and we are all weary and that makes us say things we do not mean.'

'But I do mean it!' I said. 'I never say things I do not mean. Never. Ever.'

And with that I went out and slammed the door behind me.

What was happening to me? Hadn't my father just showed signs that he might get better after all? Wasn't my mother fair worn out with looking after him? Hadn't she lost yet another of her precious babies? Wasn't Joseph working hard, learning a trade so that he might put food on the table? And wasn't Father a man and the best man I ever did know?

I ran down to the Cobb. Harry and three other fishermen were working on their boats ready for the spring, painting on the sticky black pitch that would stop the water getting in.

'Well, if it isn't little Miss Anning come to pay us a visit!' said Harry, his blue eyes twinkling. 'How's Father Anning this fine day?'

'He spoke. He spoke to me!' I burst out, and then suddenly I was crying and crying and crying as if I would never stop.

Harry put down his brush and wiped his hands on his overalls. I thought he might try to hug me but he knew me better than that, it seemed. He ruffled my hair just as my father used to before he had his accident.

'Tis the way of it,' he said kindly. 'While tis all gloom and doom and sorrow, we show a brave face to the world and go about our business as if all is well. Then, when it is all well at long last, all the sorrow we have kept at bay . . . just as the

Cobb keeps back the storms ... all that sorrow comes flooding over us, all of a sudden. You, young Mary, you can scarce believe your grief is over and that is why you cry. Tis the way of it,' he said again, giving my hair one last ruffle.

I dried my eyes and my runny nose on my sleeve and stood up as straight-backed as I could, which made my bodice feel very tight indeed, I must say. He was right. It made no sense at all, but he was right. We had all been hiding our sorrow, trying to pretend all would be well. Now it would be!

'Thank you. And thank you for all the salt fish. It helped. And my eel skull. It is my favourite possession, apart from my necklace and my hammer, and I am showing it to Father tomorrow.'

'Good girl!' Harry smiled approvingly before taking up his brush again and returning to his task. 'You're a good little maid, for all you are a strange one.'

Harry was a good man. And so too was Henry. Maybe I would get a letter from him after all. The thought of it warmed me a bit and I headed back for home a little lighter in my step and in my heart until I reminded myself that, if a letter were to come, it would be I who must pay for it. Let no letter come, then, for there was no money for such fripperies. Was there no end to the deprivations of we poor?

13

A REMINDER AND
A REMEMBRANCE

*A*fter that day when Father spoke to me at long last, he slowly, slowly began to look more like his old self again. The yellowed skin turned white and then pink; the bones which showed through gradually disappeared from sight again; his shaggy mane of knotted hair was washed and cut and his beard trimmed.

He moved about slowly at first, clinging to one of us or leaning against the wall as he made his way around the house. He sat for long hours by the back door, taking in the weak early spring sunshine, and seeming to read pamphlets about God and the Church and Science. It seemed that the church people had not turned him from his Dissenter ways, for all they tried so hard. They would not have liked these writings, with their talk of not everything in the Bible being actual truth or of it being good to use science to help understand how the world was created. They were not very exciting to read and Father seemed to feel the same way for I never saw him turn a page, so I am sure he was just pretending to read them. The smile I had seen that day he spoke for the first time since his fall had not been seen again.

Sometimes I sat with him, picking over a pail of muddy stones which I had brought up from Black Ven in the hope of entertaining him and rekindling the interest he had once had, but he never so much as looked.

'Are you afear'd to go back out there, Father?' I asked one day, as we sat together. He was daydreaming; I was turning two crocodile teeth over and over in my hands and thinking with half my head about whether they were not teeth at all but maybe bones.

He stayed silent, staring straight ahead of him, down the street, as if transfixed by something only he could see.

'Well?' I persisted. 'Are you? Afear'd? Because I be not afear'd. I go alone and I could take you with me, if you are. You could bring your stick and lean on me when the path gets stony or steep, and sit upon the rocks and spy out likely finds.'

But he did not answer. Only stared.

'Have you gone deaf, Father?' I asked, pulling at his sleeve. It seemed as if he was a thousand, thousand miles away. He put his hand up to his head where the scar showed in a raised white line, like the worm trail on a mussel shell. 'Does your head hurt, still?'

Still no reply.

There wasn't much purpose in talking to a person who wouldn't answer. I fell to wondering. Could a person stop being the same person and become someone else? He looked like my father. He smelled like my father (which was a very good thing as that stinking creature in his sickbed had not been nice to be close to at all). Yet, somehow, he was not himself. Not Father. Just like an empty shell, the creature in it long gone, eaten by a gull maybe, so he was eaten up by his ailment, such that nothing of him remained except the body he'd lived in.

A sudden wave of anger came over me. What was the point of him being spared if he was of no use to man nor beast? What was his purpose if all he did was sit in silence or eat our scant food or pass away the hours in bed? There was work he could be doing and money he could be earning. There wasn't even any entertainment to be had from him! He was neither interesting nor interested. We had been so happy, so joyful that he had recovered from the fall, but that happiness, that joy had faded, truth to tell. I began to ponder whether it might not have been better had he died for he had wasted so much of our time and effort and grief and all to have him sit on the step in the sun, saying not a word.

I gave him a poke in his ribs, which still stuck proud like

the hull of a wreck. He gave a thin wail of pain but still did not look at me.

'Father!' I said, as fiercely as I could. 'You have to stop this nonsense now. I know tis not my place to berate you, but we have all suffered for long enough. Tis time you did . . .' And here I hesitated for I was about to say a very rude thing indeed which I had heard a rough woman say to her drunken husband: *'Tis time you did do your business or get off the pot!'*

There. I'd said it. I had not understood what the woman had meant at the time for her husband was not on the pot, him being in the street at the time, but now I saw it clear. It was a way to say 'Pull yourself together or give up!' and that is what I wanted Father to understand. He could not be a burden to us or to himself a moment longer.

I watched his face for signs that he had heard. A little tear welled up in the corner of one eye and rolled down through the lines in his cheek and vanished into his beard. It was like watching a raindrop go down a window pane. It seemed to take for ever. But I could not feel sorry for him. I had no sorrow left.

I was close to poking him again when, of a sudden, a slow, small smile spread across his face as, still staring ahead, he reached out for my hand and took it, squeezing hard.

'Oh, Mary!' he cried, turning to me at last. 'What a creature you are! Why, who but my little Lightning Mary could haul me out of my pit of despond? I will not ask where you learned such a phrase but, by the heavens, it hit its mark and no mistake! How right you are. It's been long enough. Long enough, indeed. I beg your forgiveness and your mother's and Joseph's. You'll have to bear with me a little longer for I am still weak but, as you say, tis time.'

It was the longest speech he had made in many a long month and it warmed my heart to hear him with something of his old resolve and spark.

'I'll help you, Father. Spring's nearly here. There are visitors in Lyme already. I can sell our curiosities whilst you make cabinets. There are customers waiting for you to return to your work, so there is money to be made if you could just get back into the workshop.'

He ruffled my hair and I felt my love for him return. 'So be it, Mary. So be it.'

And so it was. Father went back into his workshop and, though he was much weakened and very slow and had a cough which he could not shake off, he managed to make enough to keep our heads above water.

Mother started smiling again as, once more, she found herself with child. I could not be pleased, try as I might. You know how I feel on these matters. Still, it meant that our days returned to how they had been before the accident, near enough.

Then a day came that turned out to be very different indeed. Nearly a year since I had first met Henry. More than half a year since he had left Lyme.

I had started running errands for Mrs Stock, Squire Stock's wife. She had been very kind when Father was ill and had taken it upon herself to try to put paid work our way. I was happy enough to visit the stores and the market on her behalf and she profited from my skill at bargaining so, though she paid me pennies and sometimes shillings, I cost her very little if anything at all by the savings I made. Her husband owned a fair bit of land hereabout and Father, as I have told you, had made furniture for them before. Mrs Stock is a short, bustling sort of woman, always in a hurry and always talking at a very great rate. I let most of what she says wash over me like a wave over a pebble. Of course, I pay attention to instructions. Anyway, on this particular day, she seemed more animated than ever and beamed at me and pinched my cheeks as she told me to run along up to the top of Silver Street and call on Mrs De la Beche.

My heart stopped for what seemed like minutes and I stared at Mrs Stock with my mouth open like a stranded mackerel.

At last I said, 'And what am I to do there, ma'am? Must I take or collect something for you?'

At this, she looked very pleased with herself and pinched

my cheeks again. 'No, child. There is nothing to collect for me! It is *you* who have something to collect! And it will cheer you most marvellously! I am confident of that! After all the heartache you have had, you deserve some good thing to happen to you! Now, run along! The sooner you go, the sooner you may have your— Ah! But let it be a surprise for you, my dear Mary!'

With that, she gave my cheeks one last pinch and winked at me before turning away and disappearing down the street.

So. A letter from Henry at long last. That was all it could be. It was good of him to take measures to ensure that I would not have to bear the cost of its delivery, and very sensible too, since if it had been delivered to Cockmoile Square, I should have been obliged to refuse to take it, which would have been very vexing indeed.

So I set off up the hill to Silver Street and the house of the sugared buns, though I doubted very much there would be any buns for me that day. I opened the big wrought-iron gate and went up the driveway to the front door. For a moment, I hesitated, wondering if it might not be better to go round the side to the tradesmen's entrance, but I was not a tradesperson, at least not officially, and I had gone in the front door with Henry so I should do so again.

I pulled the rope on the ship's bell that hung by the door and waited, excited by the prospect of a letter.

Nothing. Silence. I took hold of the knocker and gave the door a thoroughly good bashing. Still nothing. Had Mrs Stock sent me on a wild goose chase? I put my ear to the door and nearly fell headlong into the hallway when a woman of about Mother's age and dressed all in black silk opened it. I recovered myself quickly and looked her up and down.

'You are very smartly dressed for a maid,' I said, 'but then, I suppose they treat you well because they are so very much against slavery, though they have a cook as well, so perhaps they like servants well enough and tis nothing but humbug.'

The woman tried to hide a smile which I thought rather impertinent since I was a visitor after all.

'I am here to see Mrs De la Beche at the request of Mrs Stock. Please be so good as to tell her I am here.' This is how fancy folk announced themselves when they deigned to visit Father's workshop. I pulled myself up to my full height and wished my skirts did not lift to show my knees but it could not be helped.

'Why!' said the woman, near to laughter as far as I could tell. 'You have told her yourself! You must be the famous Miss Anning Henry talks of so often. Welcome, Mary. I may call you Mary?'

I was rather annoyed to have been put on the wrong foot

as it were. 'A person should not pretend to be another person. You might have told me. Why do you answer your own door? It isn't normal.'

At this she laughed out loud. 'Ah, dear child. Henry told me that I would find you strong of will and plain of speech and how right he was! We keep no maids here, Mary, only Cook, and she is more of an old family friend than a servant, so I hope you can see that we do not indulge in humbug. Come, I have a letter for you.'

She turned and swept into a large room full of comfortable chairs, a settle and a grand piano.

'Sit down, Mary. Would you like a cup of tea?'

'That I would! And a sugared bun too, thank you.' The words were out of my mouth before I could stop them.

She laughed again and a question came into my head with such force that I could not help myself.

'Are you still mourning for your husband? Only my father very near died months ago but now he is well again, to a degree, but I would not still be grieving if he had died. But then again, you do laugh a lot so you cannot be altogether sad, can you? Oh, and did sharks really eat the sailors when they were drowning and was the sea red with blood? Henry told me all about the shipwreck but I did wonder if some of it might not be real, just showing off, which he does do, mainly with Joseph but sometimes—'

I checked myself for I could feel the torrent of words and questions threatening to overwhelm me as they do when my head is full and I have said nothing out loud for a long time, which I hadn't.

She looked sad for a moment and then she clapped her hands together in her lap and leaned towards me. 'Well, Mary. Since we are speaking frankly, I will tell you how it is. I *am* mourning my husband, but I am mourning Henry's absence more, even though he spent almost every waking hour out with you. I'll let you into another secret, one woman to another. This is my most comfortable, most luxurious dress and I fancy black rather suits me, don't you? So, I wear it to please myself and no one else. I am sure you can understand that, Mary?'

'Well, I have no choice as to what I wear as you may see for yourself.' I tugged at my skirts in an effort to cover my knees which I could see now were rather dirty and covered in scratches and bruises from kneeling on rocks. 'But is it true about the sharks? And did the sailors want to eat Henry?'

Again that tinkly laugh. 'Mary, Mary! What a tonic you are!' she tapped the side of her nose with one finger before she added, 'To be honest and, again, between you and me, I think Henry might have been ever so slightly guilty of exaggeration, no doubt to impress you! There were hungry sharks, yes, and hungry sailors too, but neither got much more than ship's biscuits! Now. Here is your letter.' She took an envelope from the mantelpiece and handed it to me. 'You can read it while I make some tea. I can make tea, you know! Cook is away today but she has left a very fine plum cake. Perhaps you would like a slice now and then you can take the rest home?'

I nodded my head vigorously, but all my attention was on breaking the seal on the letter which was addressed to me in Henry's neat hand.

I had never, ever had a letter of my very own.

The paper unfolded like a map. There in the middle was a very funny drawing of Henry on a horse, looking very fine in his uniform, except that he was sitting the wrong way, facing the tail and the poor beast was looking round at his bottom in shock or horror.

He had labelled the drawing in the same way he labelled our finds:

> *'Henry De la Beche, Cavalry cadet in full fig.'*
>
> *'Horse: Troy. A fine fellow who is not best pleased to have said cadet as his master. Has been known to bite cadet's bottom.'*
>
> *'Note cadet's riding position fails in one vital element. Can the scientist identify the flaw?'*

The letter itself was quite short.

Dear Mary,

I hope that by now I am forgiven. Lord knows, I have been punished enough. This is no life for me. I am like a fish out of water as you may see from the diagram above. Some of your wilfulness seems to have infected my spirit for I am constantly in trouble for insubordination and for speaking my mind. If you do not know what insubordination is, do not ask Mother as it will only alarm her, but I rather think you do.

I did.

I continued to read.

Am I trying to make them throw me out of college? Perhaps. It is a dangerous strategy for it will disappoint Mother and spoil my prospects but I cannot believe that I was put on this Earth to be a soldier.

Enough of me. I heard from Mother who heard from Cook that your father has been very gravely ill. I am very sorry for him, for you, for your whole family. I have asked Mother to help and I believe she has enlisted Mrs Stock, for Mother does not go out about town much.

Please write and tell me how you are and how the science is progressing and about your father too. Mother will give you pen and paper, if you need them.

130

We did not part as friends, for which I am eternally sorry, but I hope we might one day meet again and you will find me still, as before, your obedient servant and fellow scientist.

As I folded up the letter, Mrs De la Beche re-entered the room with a tray which she set down on a little table by her chair.

'Is he well?' she asked. 'I have not had a letter myself for some days now.'

I was pleased she did not ask me if he was subordinate as I now knew him to be very insubordinate.

'He is.'

I hoped she would not ask more questions and she seemed to understand.

'Do not let me forget to give you some writing materials when you leave. If you would like some?'

'I would. Thank you.'

All my words had dried up as the Marys in my head started to think of all manner of things and wanted to be left alone to do so. Science. Friendship. Father. Mrs Stock. Henry. My obedient servant! Quite right too!

I smiled to myself and then began to eat the cake that Henry's mother had offered me and which I had taken without paying it or her any attention at all.

14
BLOOD

*N*ot long after my eleventh birthday, which passed without celebration, I was running an errand for some sprats for Mrs Stock (for her *cat*, to be more truthful! There's poor folk, poorer even than us, who would eat a cat let alone a sprat!) when I saw a crowd of people gathered at the end of the Cobb. I could not resist going to see what they were gawping at. It was low tide, so maybe some fool had fallen in the ooze and couldn't get out.

As I got closer, I could see bigwigs and their ladies pointing and pulling faces, the ladies with their lace kerchiefs over their mouths and noses. Then I saw what they found so disgusting. Hanging from the mast of one of the boats was the body of a dead horse, strung up by its hind leg. Its skin had been peeled off it so that the meat underneath shone pink in the sun. Fishermen were hacking chunks off it for bait.

The smell was vile, so for once I could understand the

ladies being so fussy. I could not help but be fascinated, though, monstrous though the sight and the stench were. I had not seen a whole carcass like this before. I could see the big slabs of muscle across the beast's haunches, shoulder and neck. Smaller strands of white stretched between the joints. I divined that these were like the strings of a puppet, allowing the animal to move by lifting hooves, bending knees. The fishermen had stripped one leg completely and it dropped to the deck in a clatter of bones and a splatter of blood.

One of the ladies went into a swoon and was just caught before her head hit the cobbles. Why she watched if she had no stomach for such things, I had no idea. Agreed, I too was observing but I was being a scientist. She was taking pleasure at the sight of a dead creature or just frightening herself with blood and gore. Either way, it was not a good reason to be there. Such things are not entertainment but there is no accounting for the strange tastes of these London folk.

I moved closer so that I could study the body more closely. I had seen from my father's case how a body diminished when the flesh was stripped off it through illness and that should have come as no surprise. After all, the eel's skull was much smaller than the creature itself had been when it was alive and a fish skeleton gives few clues as to how much meat it provided before it was cooked and eaten. All the Marys in my head started running around having ideas about the curiosities and how bones held together and how many bones might be in a body and how big that body might really be with the meat and guts and skin all back where they should be. I wished I had brought paper and pen with me so that I could make a scratch for Henry.

I was lost in my thoughts entirely, so I fair jumped out of my own skin when I was tapped on my shoulder.

A man stood behind me. I thought I might have seen him somewhere else but, before I could fathom out where, he announced himself to be the very Mr De Luc who had admired Henry's sketches last summer.

'Ah! I see you have progressed from fossicking to the study of anatomy! A macabre subject for a young lady, I must say!'

'Firstly, I do not know what ana-whatever you said is. Secondly I do not know what "mackarb" is. Thirdly, I am not a young lady, as I am sure you are well aware. Perhaps you would care to explain?' I might as well learn some new words while I was about it. I could put them in my letter and that would give Henry something to think about!

'Anatomy. *A-na-toh-mee*. It's the study of the structures of organisms . . . living creatures . . . and how they work. And macabre? Well, that means . . . I do not know the English word . . . maybe gruesome? Something disturbing to do with death? And you are a young lady to anybody who is

134

a gentleman and I consider myself to be one such. Does that satisfy you?'

'It does. I am a scientist more than anything, though.' I said this in hushed tones, confident that none could hear me.

He raised his eyebrows at this. Why do adults always do this with me? It is most vexing!

I continued more forcefully, 'I am a scientist so I must study all manner of things.' Then it struck me that he might be useful again. 'If people find a horse bone or an eel skull or a sheep's jaw, they can tell what it was when it was alive because they have seen it alive. Do you think a person might be able to tell what a creature was even if they had never seen that creature living? In fact, if *no one* had seen it living?'

He pulled at his long moustache and twisted the ends into a point. 'That should, indeed, be possible but I think you would have had to have seen a very great number of creatures to have enough of the information you would need to make what is, let us be very frank here, my dear young lady, a guess as to what the unknown creature might be or how it looked. Perhaps I might suggest that only one who had observed and rebuilt many skeletons might be able to come by such knowledge.' He paused. 'I must assume that you are speaking of your "curiosities"?'

'I might be,' I said cautiously, for I did not want him

135

stealing my ideas, and I also wanted to think about what he had said about other skeletons. 'Are you a scientist?'

He looked very pleased with this question. 'I am. I pursue a science to which, I am rather proud to say, I have given a name. No, not De Luc. I call it "geology"—'

'The study of the Earth,' I interrupted him. 'My friend Henry is a geologist. Well, he will be. He's being insubordinate on a horse at the moment, but he will be a geologist when he has finished that.'

Mr De Luc seemed to think this was highly amusing and it was, especially if you had seen Henry's funny drawing.

'Well! My word! What a knowledgeable young lady you are! It is my honour, mademoiselle, to be reacquainted. I wish you well in your studies! You must attend a very enlightened school.'

'Oh, I don't go to school any more, not since my father had his accident. Besides, I only went on Sundays to learn my letters and such but there's neither money nor time for school now. I have to make my own studies when and where I may.'

The gentleman looked gravely but kindly upon me. 'I am sorry to hear that your father met with an accident. I trust he will make a full recovery. You are clearly a young woman of enterprise and intellect and I look forward to reading many an expert pamphlet on your discoveries!'

With that he tipped his hat and walked away down the Cobb and back towards town.

So! I am a woman of enterprise and intellect! Another story for Henry, and a most productive day indeed.

I tore myself away from the poor horse and the crowds and went to get Mrs Stock's cat's sprats. I saved her a penny or two as Mr Samways gave me a handful of fish he had dropped in the sawdust while arranging his wares. I washed them off under the town pump and they were like new, if a little mangled. The cat would have to put up with that, fussy creature.

When I got to Mrs Stock's house, which was a walk of more than two miles up Red Lane, she was in her garden, sorting out the canes for her runner beans.

She stood up, smiling, as she saw me approach. 'Mary, child! I wondered what had happened to you! You have Zebediah's supper?'

I held up the little packet which had been leaking fishy water all the way up the path.

'Good girl. He will thank you for it.'

I doubted that very much since Zebediah was not, as far as I knew, the first-ever talking cat.

'So much to do and the time just flies by,' she continued, as she gathered up her scissors and the ball of twine with which she had lashed the canes together. 'And look at you! Growing up so fast!'

Everyone kept on so about me growing up. What benefit there was to growing up, I could not work out for the life of me. I was suffering mightily from the tightness of my clothes, I knew that.

Mrs Stock must have seen my discomfort. 'I have been thinking for some time now that we need to get you some clothes more befitting a young lady! Now, Mary, don't you scowl so! I know your taste! I would not dare to suggest sprigged muslins, even though I hear it is quite the latest fashion! Oh, I see you wrinkle your nose! Worry no more. I will find you some plain old workaday dress of mine in grey or brown and then you will be happy. Is that not so?'

Mrs Stock did indeed know my tastes, it seemed. I followed her inside and began to climb the stairs behind her.

She turned. 'Mary! Not with the fish! Put it in the pantry and mind you close the door or that naughty Zebediah will help himself!'

Zebediah was a very large, very fat, ginger cat with a chewed ear and a pink nose. He was not friendly at all. I cannot see the point of keeping a beast that bites and scratches and has to be fed sprats because it is too fat and too lazy to catch a mouse or a rat. He was curled up by the range, even though it was a warm day. He opened one eye as I came into the room and then that pink nose of his twitched and he was up on his feet fast as you like and winding himself around my legs as I tried to get to the pantry, so that I was obliged to kick him several times. This bothered him not at all. But then he saw me toss the fish onto a shelf and shut the door, quick as a flash, before he had a chance to rush in himself. In an instant, he turned from the false friend to an angry foe, growled and took a swipe at my legs with his claws, drawing blood.

'You evil fiend!' I hissed at him, copying his ways, but he stared back at me with his great yellow eyes as if nothing had happened and returned to his spot in front of the range. 'Spoiled brat of a cat that you are!' I finished. He took to washing himself, sticking his hind leg out as if he were a dancer. I quite admired him for that indifference – nothing like a dog which must always be petted and praised. Maybe I was more like a cat than a dog, though I do not care for sprats or to be too hot.

'Mary!' Mrs Stock's voice came from somewhere up above. 'Mary! I have just the thing for you!'

I licked my finger, wiped the beads of blood off my leg and went upstairs to find her. I am sure Mrs Stock liked her house very well and it must be most pleasant to have a comfortable bed and a room to oneself but, oh, the fussiness of it all! Bits and bobs and china on every piece of furniture and barely an inch of wall that was not covered in portraits of families and children and cats. It made my head quite giddy, so much was there to see. I followed the sound of her voice into a big room in which stood a very large wardrobe, the work of my father, I noted with pride.

Mrs Stock held out two dresses, one in a dark green, the other in a pale grey. Both looked serviceable enough to me.

'Try them on, Mary! I can get them altered to fit you if they are too big for I am so much fatter than you will ever be! Just as well I am not the tallest of women, though! Isn't that lucky?'

I did not really care if they were too large. I just wanted a garment to cover me up and hide my knees to stop folk laughing at me, and something I could breathe in without fearing that all the seams might burst.

'You will grow into a fine young woman, Mary,' continued Mrs Stock. 'Very strong and capable. You are no great beauty, tis true, but you'll make some man a very fine wife, to be sure, give it three or four years.'

I growled under my breath, somewhat like Zebediah. 'I am only eleven years old. Why must people always be talking about getting wed? Tis all I ever hear!' I imitated their wheedling voices. '"*You'll be wed soon!*" "*You'll have babbies of your own!*" Well, I won't.'

Mrs Stock patted my arm. 'Now, now. I did not mean to upset you. You are right. You are young, yet. Tis easy to forget, Mary, for you are so old and wise beyond your years in so many ways. You've had a lot to bear, with your father's accident and your mother so often ill herself and with child again. Now. Try this dress on and we'll have no more talk of growing up. You've time enough for that, I daresay. Now, let's see how you look in the green dress! Off with that old thing!'

She did not look away as I struggled to take off my dress without my shift coming off with it. Things were happening to my body. Things I did not like. Things I did not wish her or anybody to see. I put the green dress on as quickly as I could. It was big, too big, but it hid my body and it did feel nice to be in a dress that did not squeeze or scratch, for the cloth was a fine, soft worsted wool, worn from washing. It was also plenty long enough but not so long as to trip me up. It would last a long time.

'Take a look in the mirror, Mary. See what you think.'

What did I think? That was a question! I stared at my reflection. My face looked very white and pinched. I was certainly no beauty, but what of it? I could hear and see and speak as well as anyone and Mr De Luc had called me a woman of enterprise and intellect and Henry had called me a genius so what else were a head and face for? Not an adornment, for sure. A vessel for my brain, no more, no less.

The dress hung shapelessly from my shoulders so that my anatomy (I was proud to use the word) could not be seen and only the tips of my boots were visible instead of my grazed and bruised knees.

Mrs Stock was watching me closely. I could see her in the glass as she stood behind me. She spoke very quietly, almost under her breath, as if she did not want anyone else to hear, which was strange as there was no one in the house but we two.

'Your mother will have told you about becoming a woman, I am sure. Oh, I know, we said we'd have no more talk of growing up and I will say only this. You know, I hope, that you may always ask me anything, Mary. You do know that, don't you? Lord knows, I have had daughters enough myself to make me quite the expert. So do not be shy.'

Whatever did she mean? She seemed to suggest there was some great secret with her confidential tones and her offer of advice. And what was there to know about being grown up but that you had to get married and have babies? I had heard little else from Mother for the last year or more. Yet something about this conversation made me uneasy and I turned my attention to the other dress, picking at the buttons to distract myself.

Mrs Stock took it from me and folded it up. 'I think we can say that this one will be satisfactory too. I could take them both in so that they fit you a little better, but I sense that is not your wish?'

I nodded.

'Mrs De la Beche asks after you,' she said, at last changing the subject as she folded up my old frock. 'Poor lady. She has had a hard life and no mistake. You are both missing young Henry, I am sure. Maybe you could visit her again? I think she would like it.'

'Maybe,' I said. 'I am very busy.'

I nearly said that I had science work to do, but science was still a dangerous word to use with those who thought it ungodly so I said no more and neither did she.

When I got home, Mother nodded her approval but Joseph laughed and said I looked like a wooden spoon poking out of a sack, a comment I found more comforting than insulting.

Father said nothing. I told him about the horse and he just said that he had seen it too. He was not interested to hear more so I did not tell him about the Swiss gentleman.

There was no mistaking it. Father was becoming unwell again. It pained me to think it and I had long been trying to put it from my mind. But the truth could be denied no longer. The past few weeks had seen him grow pale, with great purplish-black shadows under his eyes. He was getting thinner. Bones showed through his skin as they had last winter. He coughed. Sometimes he went into a fit of coughing for several minutes. These fits left him weak and seemingly wracked with pain.

I observed that Mother always watched him closely when he had these spells and I started watching too. I knew what she was looking for.

Blood.

Blood on the rag he put to his mouth. Blood on the bed where he laid his head. Blood on the rough linen shift.

We all knew what that meant.

The wasting disease. Consumption.

Death.

Some got better, it was true, but most did not. I thought back to that day I had almost stepped on Amy Martin's grave. She had been joined by tens of others since then. Would Father soon be under the earth? Why had the Lord spared him if only to take him away again? For the baby that would be born before Christmas? For Joseph? For me? There was no sense in it.

At that moment, Father fell to coughing as if my thinking of it had made it happen. He twisted and groaned as the violence of the cough tore through his chest. He was blind to us, deaf to our concern. He writhed like an eel on a spike.

I felt my fists forming into tight balls and I thumped my own sides as hard as I could. I felt tears of fury, hot in my eyes.

Then, just as suddenly as it had begun, the coughing stopped. Father sat on a stool, hunched over his knees, clutching his head. His breath came out in ragged gasps. After a few moments, he stood up.

'Sorry. Must have got a bit of dust in my throat. All's well now.'

It was a lie. I knew it was a lie. I glanced at Mother. She shook her head and carried on with her task, darning one of Father's stockings as if nothing had happened.

'So, Mary!' He was animated again, like the Father of old. 'Tell me again what it was made you want to look at that poor dead horse, eh? Are you a little ghoul, my little streak of lightning?' And then he looked at me in my new old dress. 'Well! Look at you in your finery! Come and give your old father a hug, there's a good girl!'

He held me tightly and I smelled that sour smell again. I was afraid. I was angry. More angry than anything else. Did we have to go through all that turmoil all over again?

That night, I prayed as hard as I could. I prayed that Father would be spared. I offered God a deal. Spare my father and let me suffer some consequence or let him die quickly and in little pain. Anything but the turning upside down of our lives to no good purpose.

The next morning, there was blood on the front of his shirt and blood on the back of my nightgown as if I had sat on a gutted fish. It seemed that God intended for us both to die.

15
MOTHER BREAKS HER SILENCE

*B*y midday I had blood on my nether garments, coming from I knew not where precisely, only that it was shameful and frightening and that I had a gnawing pain deep in my belly as if a rat was chewing on my entrails.

What if I bled to death? What if the Lord was punishing me for saying I was a scientist? What if I had made a pact, not with God, but with the Devil? I took one of the napkins Mother used for the babies and tried to staunch the bleeding. I also tried to wash out my nightdress and drawers without Mother seeing, but she caught me in the yard, scrubbing with all my might at the stain.

She pulled me away from the pail and into her arms. She kissed the top of my head and said softly: 'Oh, Mary. My little Mary. Are you all so growed up now? I must welcome you to the blessings and the woes of womankind, poor child . . . or woman, as I must call you now.'

I pulled away from her and went back to my scrubbing. 'Am I to die?' I muttered. 'Or have a baby?'

'Lord, no! Tis just nature. You have become a woman is all!'

'Why did you not warn me?' I asked through gritted teeth, as all the Marys in my head started to run about, squawking like headless chickens.

'I had not thought t'would be so soon, you being more like to a boy than a girl in your ways, but it seems that will not spare you a woman's burden. God grant you a woman's joy one day. You will see tis a price worth paying.' She ran her hand tenderly over the growing curve of her stomach.

I felt a fury in me then. I scrubbed and scrubbed as hot tears ran down my cheeks and joined the reddened water in the pail.

'Come!' said Mother, gently pulling at me. 'Leave those clothes to soak. You'll wear a hole with your scrubbing. Come and sit with me and let me tell you how it will be for you.'

I shook her off. 'I have but one question. Will it stop? Or shall I bleed to death?'

'It will stop. But it will come again every month just the same, unless you are with child, until ye be too old to bear children and then it will stop entirely.'

'Then I wish to be old now. I wish it to stop *now*!'

'I know, Mary. I know. Tis hard when first it comes but it is nature's way and we must accept it for there is nothing we can do to stop it save for being with child. One day, Mary, one day you may wish to have babbies of your own.'

I turned on her. '*Why?* Why must it always be about babbies and husbands and doing the will of men! Why? Is there never to be talk of anything else? Is that all the life I have before me? Is that all I will ever be? *Why?* Why was I spared death by the lightning strike if it was just for this? It is unjust! And what of men? Do they bleed? I see by your face that they do not! Why is it women suffer so?'

She stroked my head. 'Tis all creatures of our sex, Mary. Tis nature, as I told you. Men pay their dues in other ways. Lord knows, your poor father is paying a heavy price.'

'He brought it on himself, you said. His accident? He brought it on himself! Did *I* bring this upon myself? Did I *ask* to be a woman? I did not. I hate it! I hate these!' I banged my chest. 'I hate babies and husbands and men and being poor and the sickness and the toil and the injustice! What have we done? Why are we to be punished so? Why? And what about Father? I tried to make a pact with God but he did not listen. He just sent me blood and sent Father blood too. Much the Lord cares about the likes of we! It is unjust! It is unfair!'

148

Mother looked at me sorrowfully. 'Whoever told you that life was fair, Mary? Not I. It is what it is. We must make of it what we will and be thankful for such kindness and mercy as is bestowed upon us.'

'And should we be thankful if God takes Father from us? And that we shall be left alone, with yet another mouth to feed? Are we to be grateful for that?'

'We must accept what we may not change, Mary. You must be content with your lot on this Earth, or you will be unhappy, for it is not going to change no matter how hard you wish it. Come! I'll make you a special drink that will ease your cramps.'

'I don't want a special drink! I just want this to all go away!' I cried, and I pushed past Mother and ran out of the square and up the road to the church. As I ran through the graveyard I stamped on the ground as hard as I could and shouted to the gravestones: 'You are free. More free than I shall ever be until I be in the ground with you!'

I was crying. My hair was in my eyes. The pain was worse and I felt that, whatever Mother said, I would surely die. Where better to end my days than on this shore and by this sea that had wanted to take me into its depths for so long?

Just as I reached the little gate to the path, I suddenly remembered Henry's sketchbook. The memory of it hit me as hard as any blow. I wiped the tears from my eyes and the snot from my nose with my sleeve and took the book from its hiding place in the wall. It was just as it had been all those months ago, a little curled from damp perhaps, but in the main unspoiled.

I clutched it to me and slid down to my haunches with my back to the wall and there I stayed for an hour or more, my head full of pain and sorrow and anger.

When my passion had subsided and my headache eased, I began to leaf through the pages and recall to mind each day of that summer. There were his little maps, his intricate drawings of serpents and scuttles and then another picture. One I had not seen before and the sight of which seemed to stop my heart for a second. A dark scene, dusk maybe. The cliff shapes were black against the deep gloom of the sky. In the centre, a figure striking a rock with a hammer, again black against the sky. Splitting that sky in two jagged halves, a bolt of lightning with its point touching the head of the figure.

Beneath the drawing, Henry had written: *Lightning Mary. Scientist and Friend.*

Lightning Mary. The secret, private name that only my father used. Henry must have heard my story and thought of the name himself, for I had never told him in case he thought my brains only came because of the storm, as so many did. I did not want him to think that. My mind was my mind.

I traced the letters with my finger and felt a swell of pride. 'Scientist and Friend.' Better than wife and mother any day.

Mother was making bread when I returned home. A cup of pinkish water stood waiting for me.

'It's gone cold,' she said, not looking up from her kneading, 'but I daresay it will work almost as well. Raspberry leaf.'

I drank it down. It was bitter and had not much taste of raspberry.

'And here, take these.' She gestured to the deep pocket in her apron for me to help myself as her hands were grey with flour. 'You'll have worked out what to do with them, I'm sure. No different from the nappies, I am afraid, and the same boiling to get them clean. You'll need to change them more than once a day and don't run about or they may fall out of your drawers.'

I took out the napkins and shuddered, before stuffing them in my own pockets.

'Father will die, won't he?' This fact seemed now as clear as day in my head.

Mother slammed the dough down onto the table, sending up a cloud of flour. 'He will.'

'When?' I asked. Mother seemed so calm.

'I fear he'll not see the year out. Your blood came today. His many weeks since.'

'You didn't tell me. Why?'

She turned to look me straight in the eye. Her own were filled with tears. 'Because you were a child. Because you have long enough to be sorrowful. Because you cannot change it, and because he is precious to you and you are precious to him, and because he bade me keep silence. Now you ask me straight and I cannot hide the truth from you. We must be brave, you and I and Joseph. Braver than we have ever been. Now. Take him his dinner, Mary, and mind you say nothing of this to him. It would break his heart.'

She drew a deep breath, sighed and turned her attention back to the dough.

The route to Father's workshop took me right along the seafront and up a narrow alleyway. The town was full of visitors, promenading up and down Marine Parade, enjoying the sunshine despite the gusts of wind which came off the sea. I weaved in and out of them, ignoring their stares at my dress, which billowed like a sail.

Up at the workshop, the doors were open and a half-made cabinet stood in a shaft of sunlight, surrounded by the curls of wood that had fallen from the plane. Of Father, there was no sign.

I went round the back of the workshop to the timber store. There he was, sawing away at a large piece of oak held in a vice.

He smiled when he saw me and wiped his sweaty hands on his apron before taking his dinner from my outstretched arms. 'What has Mother got for me today, then?' he said, unwrapping the cloth.

'Food that is wasted,' I replied, before I could stop myself.

'Wasted? What do you mean, child?' He sat down on a log and bade me sit next to him. 'What has Mother been saying?'

'The truth. That you are mortal sick and will die. And soon.'

I refused to look at him. I just stared down at the shavings and started pushing them around with the toe of my boot to make a spiral, like a serpent curled up.

'Ah. I see.' He fell silent and we sat there for some moments. His dinner lay uneaten in his lap. A lump of bread, a hunk of cheese and a deep purple plum. He picked it up and started rolling it about in his hands. 'Everything dies, Mary. You of all people do know that.'

He tried to take my hand but I shook him off.

He continued, his voice soft, 'What use would it have been to tell you? T'would spoil your summer. Make you anxious.'

I was not anxious now that I knew. I was angry. But why was I so angry? Because I do not like lies? No one had lied. I had not asked Mother or Father for the truth before that day. Was it because it had taken me so long to notice, to spot the telltale signs when Mother must have seen them weeks before?

'Mother told me to say nothing to you, for it would upset you, but then it would be more lies between us,' I said. 'Besides, Henry said it is better to be able to say goodbye before a person dies. I have to know when you are going to die so that I can say goodbye to you.'

Father began sobbing. He tried again to take my hand and this time I buried my rough hand in his rougher one. We sat for what seemed like an hour or more, our heads resting against each other. The sun moved slowly above us, until our shadows lengthened towards home.

I felt quite calm. My head was silent, peaceful.

'Best eat your dinner, Father. It will be worse wasted by you not eating it than you having it in the first place.'

Father laughed. 'My little Lightning Mary, you are quick as a flash to the nub of the matter, as ever! What a creature you are!' He broke off a lump of cheese and gave it to me, while he gnawed on the bread, which had gone even harder in the sun.

'Did you tell Henry your special name for me, my Lightning Mary name?' I asked, remembering the sketch.

He looked puzzled. 'Not I. Never spoke to the boy. Seemed a good-enough sort. Good friend to you, was he?'

'He was. He is.'

Father smiled and squeezed my hand. 'That's good. But be careful, mind. When you are growed up, things change. People stick to their own kind.'

'We are the same kind. We are both scientists. We made a pact. I know he will keep it, when he can stop being a soldier.'

'Well, Mary. All I say is, be careful. People change. They do not always keep their promises. Folks like us aren't always treated fair. Don't hope too much, there's my girl. I don't want to be looking down on you, seeing you unhappy. It never does any good to depend on another body for your happiness. You must find that in yourself. Do you understand? I see you pull a face when I say happiness. Well, you may be right. Maybe happiness is not for the likes of us, but we can find contentment, can't we? I have seen contentment in your face when you are finding treasures. Isn't that right?'

I nodded. 'It is my métier,' I said, recalling Henry's word.

Father laughed uproariously and then he started to cough.

And cough.

He bent over double, pushing me away from him as he did so. 'Don't come close, Mary,' he gasped between coughs. 'Don't come close.'

Blood flew from his mouth and struck the dirt. He seemed to be fighting to get air in his lungs. His face turned waxen and then grey and he collapsed onto the ground and was silent save for the harsh rasp of his breath.

I tried with all my might to rouse him, but he had gone where neither my voice nor my shaking could reach him.

Help. I needed to get help.

I ran down to the seafront. Visitors everywhere. No one I knew. I needed someone strong. Someone who looked as if they would not mind getting bloody or dirty.

A broad-shouldered man caught my eye and I ran up to him.

At first he looked at me in horror and his wife almost hid behind him. I suppose she thought I might want to rob them, but why she would think I'd choose the biggest man in Lyme Regis that day, I do not know.

I begged him to come with me.

'It's my father. He's fallen senseless. He's ill. Dying! Dead by now, maybe.'

The man looked confused. 'And what do you want from me?'

His wife was still shrinking beside him, clinging on to his arm.

'What do you think!' How stupid some people are! 'I need you to help carry him home!'

'It may be a ruse!' twittered the wife, in her silly high-pitched squeak of a voice.

But the man disentangled her grip, handed her his hat and looked me in the eye. 'Come on then. Where is he?'

He turned to another gentleman close by. 'Here, you; yes, you sir. Come and help this child and her sick father.'

Between us we got Father home and into his bed. He was deathly pale and his breathing was harsh, bubbling with the blood that still issued from his mouth.

Mother thanked the men and joined me at the bedside, grim-faced. We exchanged glances. I drew myself up tall beside her. I could stay a child no more.

There we were. Two women together, facing death.

PART
TWO

16

OUR LIVES ARE
FOR EVER CHANGED

*H*enry's father had died very quickly. The fever struck, he took to his bed and, bang, a day later he was gone. Was Henry wrong? Was that swift death better? Better than this endless half-dying?

Three long months had passed and Father had hardly moved since the gentlemen had carried him up our narrow stairs and laid him on the bed.

It was so different from the last time. Last time we were all hope and determination. Now we were calm. Indifferent, almost. Mother cried sometimes but never for long. Her face was like a statue's, unchanging, stern.

Joseph went to work. People brought us food and some gave us money. Harry visited and said his goodbyes just as I had said mine. The physician came early on, paid for by Squire Stock, but Mother had the sense to send him away. 'I myself may need you more in the weeks to come,' she said. 'For there is nothing to be done for him, God save his soul.'

161

We did our chores. We kept him clean and watered. He had stopped eating long since. At first, he would try to smile or open his eyes but after the first few weeks, he did neither any more. We sat with him by turns but whether he knew we were there, I could not tell, for he never said a word.

I felt cold, hard, as if I had grown a thick, tough shell of bone or stone. I was impatient to be back on the cliff. All the time I sat with Father, I was puzzling over what the curiosities might really be, how they might have looked when they were alive. I practised making copies of Henry's drawings. I took apart the skeletons of a mouse and a seagull, drew each bone and labelled it and put the skeleton back together again, using a little of the glue from Father's workshop. I wrote to Henry and told him what I had done and drew a tiny mouse skull on one corner of the page. He did not write back.

We waited. There was nothing else to do.

One day, late in October, the minister came and asked him if he wanted to confess anything but Father stayed silent, eyes closed, mouth open, breath coming out of him with a rasp, like a bramble scratching on a wall.

Mother was but two months from her confinement and she would sit beside Father, stroking her belly and talking to the unborn child, cooing or singing to it, and I thought how very irritated I should be if I was that baby having to listen to all that twittering when I wanted just to be quiet or to be born. It seemed to soothe Mother, though, so I think she sang to herself as much as the baby.

On the tenth day of November, Mother woke earlier than usual and found Father cold. She gave one long wail and then was silent. She sat up in bed, her eyes shut, her hands cradling her belly.

Joseph ran to Father and tried to take hold of his hand but it lay stiff by his side. He laid his head on Father's chest and howled like a wild dog, while Mother stroked his hair.

I stood in the doorway and stared at Father for a while. I could see that he had quite gone, but the strange thing was that he looked more alive than he had done in many a long month. Perhaps he was at peace at last, just as folk always say of the dead.

Later, neighbours came to lay him out and shooed me away when I wanted to watch what they were doing. Men dressed in black came and bore him away, for the doctor said there was still a danger from the disease that had killed him. I thought that it was rather too late to be talking of such dangers now, when we had shared our days and nights with him for so long but, in truth, it was better that they took him out of the house.

Mrs Stock came and sat with Mother for a while and talked to her of the burial. She lent Mother a black shawl, for no dress could be found to fit her. I wore the grey frock. Mother refused to have Father buried in his one good suit of clothing so that Joseph might have something to wear at the burial, so he went into the box in his work clothes. Why give your Sunday best to the worms?

Many people came, for Father, though a 'wild one' as I overheard someone say, was much admired by folk in Lyme and beyond. They cried and hugged my mother and tried to hug me. Some left us small gifts of sugar and biscuits and even wine. Harry May came with an old fisherman's cap, filled with coins collected from all over the town. I counted the coins out at the table. Eleven shillings. No fortune, it was true, but nonetheless a very great kindness from folk with scarcely two pennies to rub together themselves.

We did not speak of Father for many days but then we did not speak of much. Joseph went to work and tried, fruitlessly, to be paid for his labours. Mother made bread, stretching across the great bulge of her belly to slam the dough down and stretch it away with the heel of her hand, then stopping to rub her back from the discomfort of standing.

I ran errands, same as ever. Some days it was as if Father had never existed. Others it seemed as though he might walk in the door at any moment. I did not like those days for they made me feel very anxious and unsettled. I didn't cry. I missed Father, of course. Joseph must have felt the same way because twice I heard him sobbing into the bedclothes. He would stop as soon as he realised I was awake and listening. One night, he turned to me angrily and asked me why I did not cry.

'Sometimes, Mary, I do believe you are unnatural. That lightning must have burned all feeling from you, for you do not seem to care that Father is dead. You are a hard creature, to be sure.'

I said nothing in reply. It was not true to say I did not care. I had felt a very great pain twice in my life: once, when Henry had gone, and then when Father had first been injured; but this seemed so long ago. As for Father dying, it seemed as though there was no more sadness left to be felt. Nothing would bring him back. I could feel no sorrow now, just unease because nothing seemed to be as it should. I like day-to-day matters to be normal or for me to have the power over them. I do not like surprises. I do not like shocks. I do not like chaos and I do not like to feel that anyone else has power over me. And now I did not like the feeling that we were waiting for something or that some great change was coming.

Then, ten days after we buried Father in the earth, some different men clad in black came calling, bearing not gifts but bills. They said they were sorry for our loss but it was plain to see they were more concerned about their own if we could not pay.

One of these grim visitors stood out, a nasty little man with black eyes like a crab's. The landlord's agent, Mr Sprague. He took great delight in drawing out a sheet of paper from his breast pocket and smoothing it out in front of Mother before pushing it towards her, a false smile on his face all the while.

'One hundred and twenty pounds!' My mother had turned white as a sheet. She clutched her belly and sat down before her legs gave way. 'No! It cannot be so! One hundred and twenty! No! No!'

But it was so. There were bills for timber, for a new saw blade, the rent on the workshop had not been paid for months and the rent on the house had been paid with borrowed money. There was the bill for the burial. The total was a sum that would take six, maybe seven or more years for a man to earn, and who could tell how much longer without Father to earn it.

'You'll have to go to the workhouse, missus, if you cannot settle,' said the crab-eyed Mr Sprague, with glee.

'Or,' said another gentleman by his side, who seemed more kindly, 'I could arrange a loan for you and at very favourable terms, dear lady. Very favourable indeed!'

I was most indignant. 'Favourable to you, maybe! Why

would anybody borrow more money to pay a debt? That is the stupidest thing I have ever heard! Where is the sense in that?'

Mr Kindly-But-Stupid started gibbering away about how he was trying to help and I kept telling him it was a stupid trick to get more money from poor folk when Mother seemed suddenly to gather her wits and her skirts about her and stood up, her belly greatly adding to the effect of a woman on the warpath. 'Thank you, Mary. I will manage this now.'

She gave them one of her blackest looks and demanded in the strongest terms that they give her the time to consider how she might settle their accounts. Then she sent them scurrying out of the house with a flea in their ear for being so shamefully cruel to a poor widow woman, great with child.

They nodded and muttered and fled. Mr Sprague had his tail between his legs, as they say.

Slamming the door behind them, Mother turned to Joseph and me. She banged on the table with the flat of her hand, closed her eyes for a moment and then stood up, straight as a ramrod.

'We must make a plan,' she told us. 'We may go down but, by God, we shall go down fighting! Tis time for the Molly Moore of old to make her return!' She had a look of iron about her as she reached for the pile of bills. 'Joseph. Go to the workshop and fetch Father's ledgers. There must be folk who owe *us* money. And make an inventory of all that is in the timber yard. We will sell that at the first opportunity. Oh, and tell that master of yours to start paying you a wage now you are of use to him. You've been asking long enough. If he will not, we must find you paid work and find it fast. You are an apprentice no more.'

Joseph nodded assent.

I looked at Mother with new respect. I had not seen her so decided and strong-willed before. She turned her gaze on me.

'As for you, miss. It pains me to say it, but if we are to get out of this hole your father has left us in, you too will need paid work. Scullery maid, perhaps.'

My heart turned cold and my head hot. 'No, Mother. No. I can make more money by selling treasures.'

Mother shook her head. 'That's fool's talk, Mary. You've listened to your father for too long!'

'Father made money! No, Mother, he did! But I can make more. I am a better tradeswoman than he. Joseph will testify. Besides you will need me here when that' – I pointed at the great mound that was her belly – 'when that is out in the world. Isn't that so? Best I can be here when you need me and treasure-hunting or selling when you do not.'

'She's right, Mother,' added Joseph. 'She can find curiosities as if she were a magician and she is even cleverer than Father at getting money out of rich folk.'

Mother sighed.

'I'll run errands too. More than ever. Please, Mother! I will have no talent for maiding as well you must know. I would only lose a position as soon as I had gained it, for speaking out of turn or some such. You know how it is with me. I'm *insubordinate*!' I was unable to hide a note of triumph as I said this.

Mother sighed again. 'Yes, indeed you are. And proud of it too, I daresay. Well, maybe you can turn your faults into virtues. Let us see. You have twelve months to prove me wrong. No more.'

'I am glad you have seen sense. I—'

'Mind you do not overstep the mark, Mary Anning,' Mother interrupted sternly. 'You'll not wrap *me* around your little finger. Now, make a start on those potatoes while Joseph fetches Father's papers. Let us see how we might resolve matters.'

We were owed money. Not enough to end our troubles by any means, but enough to keep the worst of the creditors away from our door and us out of the workhouse. Not everyone who owed money paid promptly. It seemed that the richer they were, the more high and mighty, the less likely they were to settle a bill. It took Mother almost a fortnight to collect it all in.

'Sometimes,' Mother said, through gritted teeth, 'sometimes

tis like they believe they are doing *us* the favour, nay, giving us the privilege of doing work for them and they are amazed that we should wish to be paid as well!'

She was enormous with the baby that had yet to make its way into the world and cut a fearsome figure as she hunted down our debtors. If they did not respond to a bill delivered to the tradesmen's entrance, Mother would accost them in the street or march straight up and hammer on their front door, demanding payment that very instant.

She would return, triumphant, and bang the money down on the table for me to count.

'Seems Mary might have got her skills in trade from you, Mother!' said Joseph admiringly.

'Ha! I was a match for most in Blandford market, before I met your father!' Mother laughed. 'But, truth be told, I have a new method. When I see these bigwigs squirm and wriggle and try to avoid my eye and to ignore the bill, I just say, "Do you want me to set my Mary on you?" Ooh, they be afear'd of my fierce daughter! They pay quick as you like after that!'

Joseph burst out laughing. He clapped me on the back. 'Mary the Money Monster! Quake in your boots if she comes for you!'

I am pleased to be fierce. It is useful. Father would have been proud of me but, for once, it was Mother's praise of me that made me feel ten feet tall. She winked at me and I winked back. We were allies in the war against the debt and the threat of the workhouse.

December came and brought our new brother. Named for Father, Richard was a sickly thing, much like the rest.

Mother's new-found spirit was not to be found in the wailing, whining creature and he was not long for this world. The new year had scarce begun when we buried him.

Mother did not mourn. I daresay it was a relief to us all.

17
MONSTER

*T*hat winter was hard, hard, hard. If you have never been so cold that you cannot think, you cannot know how bad cold can be. There were nights we went to sleep with no hope of waking up. Baby Richard didn't. Did it hurt? Did you just fall into a dream and then into death and the life beyond?

Some days, it hurt to be alive. Hands red raw, lips cracked and bleeding, shivering that wracked your bones. No matter how much we huddled together, we just could not get warm.

We sold what furniture we could and burned the rest, piece by piece. We slept on rags on the floor and ate our thin gruel with our bottoms near frozen to the flagstones. We did not wash. We did not change our clothes. We stank so much at first that we held our breath, but then we got so used to it that we could not smell the stink any more and, after a while, I swear, we stopped stinking altogether.

We were not alone in our suffering and people did what

they could to help, but everyone was short of victuals that winter. We were determined that Father's debts would be cleared, so we refused the lenders who prey upon the poor and starving.

Somebody must have told Henry's mother how things were for us, because when Henry wrote to say how much he sorrowed for me over the death of my father, he added that we were free to help ourselves to firewood from his mother's house. I did not go in to the house when I collected the letter. Even though I felt no shame at my state, for how could I help it, it felt wrong to step into rooms so clean that they almost shone. I went round to the back of the house, filled my basket with sticks and logs and took the letter from the cook, who also gave me a packet full of sugar buns.

I was making my way back down Silver Street with my burden, when I heard a voice calling out to me. Mrs Stock, brandishing a small parcel.

'Oh, Mary! I am so glad to catch you! I have something for you! I found it quite by chance when we visited Salisbury last week. I saw it and immediately thought of you!' She held out the package before she realised that I did not have a hand free to take her gift.

'Silly me!' she cried. 'I'll follow you home. I need to see your mother, in any event.'

'Mother does not like visitors to call with no warning!'

This was because she was ashamed to let them see how we were forced to live.

'I know, Mary. I know.' Mrs Stock patted my arm. 'I won't come in, even though it's a cold day to stand on a doorstep.'

'It's just as cold inside, so it makes no odds,' I said.

Mother was not at home. Mrs Stock said nothing as she looked around at the kitchen, bare of furniture as it was, but her dismay was plain.

I unwrapped her present. It was a book. A slim volume covered in dark red leather, the title in gold letters: *Illustrations of the Huttonian Theory of the Earth* by John Playfair.

What did that mean? Mrs Stock must have seen my bewilderment for she said: 'It's all about rocks, Mary, and I know how much you love rocks. Your poor father told me about your wish to be a scientist! He was so proud of you, you know. Anyway, I saw this book in a shop in Salisbury and my first thought was you, Mary!'

I began to read the table of contents: '*Object of a theory of the Earth. Division of minerals into stratified and unstratified.*' The words were unfamiliar to me, their meanings unknown, but I felt as if that lightning bolt passed through my body once again. All the Marys in my head were jumping up and down in excitement, impatient to start reading.

I clutched the book to me and turned to Mrs Stock.

'Thank you. Thank you.' No other words would come but she seemed well pleased and patted my arm again.

'You are a good girl, Mary. A special girl. Your father knew it. Your mother knows it. I know it.'

With that, she left me with my new treasure. I wrapped myself in a shawl and began to read.

In truth, it was very difficult to understand. There were words I had never seen before, names of stone and rock that meant nothing to me. I turned more pages and then, at last, two words jumped out at me: *Fossil Bones*. I read on hungrily: '*Of the bones buried in the looser earth*'. The words sent a thrill through my being. Turning the pages brought more wonders as I read:

'*Geology of Kirwan and De Luc.*'

I had met and spoken to Mr De Luc! Maybe Mr De Luc had indeed invented the word 'geology'? Yet it seemed that from the very first few pages of the book that Mr De Luc and Mr Hutton were at odds, arguing about science and religion.

It was very hard to understand but it seemed some people thought the Earth was shaped by water and some by fire. They called themselves Neptunists or Plutonists, and Mr Hutton was more a Plutonist though he did not want to call himself that because he thought it was a silly name.

The book did not say anything at all about God. It did not say God had made everything.

It was all about scientists arguing with each other about a theory of the Earth. Scientists arguing about religion, but not talking about God. Maybe they did not believe the words in the Bible.

I shut the book. I had to write to Henry and tell him that I owned a book on science and that it was the most frightening, difficult and exciting book in the world and that I would read it in secret and share my knowledge with him.

I searched out the last scraps of paper that I had hidden away in case Mother used them to light the stove. I wrote as fast as I could, before the daylight faded and Mother and Joseph returned. I felt as if my head might explode with thoughts and ideas and theories and the shock and joy of having science in my hands in this book! When I finished, I realised that he would never be able to read it. The handwriting was disordered, the ink smudged and so thick and wet that it had soaked holes in the paper. I scrumpled it up and, before Mother and Joseph came home, I used it to start the little fire made from Mrs De la Beche's firewood.

It blazed brightly for a few seconds, lighting up the gloomy room, and then it was gone. I had one piece of paper left. I must save it for something important.

We sat in silence after our meagre supper. I looked at Joseph, pale and bony. We had nearly let ourselves be defeated by the cold, by hunger, by Father's death. The year of our

Lord 1810 was not one we should care to remember. 1811 had not started well, with yet another baby buried. Yet something about the feel of the book safely stowed away in the folds of my dress made me sense that change was coming. Over the next few days, the feeling grew and took hold of me until I knew, with no shadow of a doubt, that the time had come again to discover what treasures the sea and the storms had laid bare.

One night, I whispered to Joseph, over Mother's snores, 'Tomorrow. Black Ven. Dawn. Yes?'

He nodded and by the moon's light, I caught a tiny glint of devilment in his eye. Maybe he felt as I did, that something big, something wondrous awaited us.

The next morning dawned grey and dank with a sea fret hanging over the town like a great net, imprisoning its catch.

'Maybe we should go another day,' Joseph said, as we stood on the doorstep, trying to spy out the church tower through the mist.

I shook my head. 'No. We must go today. I feel it in my bones. There is something out there. I know it.'

Joseph shrugged. He knew better than to try to change my mind.

The sea had been busy. She had laid claim to a goodly piece of the path beyond the church. Where it had once wound along towards Charmouth, well above the reach of the tide, it now disappeared into nothing but a heap of mud and stones, sliding into the water.

We had to pick our way along much higher up. The ground fell away sharply and it was hard to get a grip in the mud. The mist hung over us, making our clothes damp and the air thick and heavy in our lungs.

'Don't get too far ahead, Mary!' shouted Joseph. 'I can hardly see you! This is madness! How are we to find anything at all when we can't even see each other?"

Maybe it was madness, but it had to be done.

'It'll clear soon enough.'

And it did. A pale sun broke through the fret, revealing the cliff face greatly changed from my last visit.

A massive slab, as big as an upended fishing boat, had slipped down from the cliffs we called The Spittles, just before Black Ven. It had slid almost as far as the pebbles on the beach.

It was what I had hoped for. No fish scales this time, I prayed silently to myself as I approached to examine the vast slice of mud and clay and rock. All of a sudden, one layer came loose and fell towards us. We waited to see if more would follow, hardly daring to breathe, but all was still.

'This whole piece may topple over yet,' Joseph warned. 'Let me try to break it up with the pick first. Then it will be safer for us both.'

He swung the pick and gradually the slab fell into smaller pieces. They looked like black gravestones and maybe that was what they were – the gravestones of creatures trapped within the mud.

By my reckoning, we had seven hours before it would be dark again. Time enough to find something.

We worked away in silence, some two yards apart, both completely absorbed by our labours. Soon, we both had a fair-sized pile of small finds – the creatures we habitually found day in, day out. Nothing of any great merit or value. Our hands were almost frozen with the cold, our mittens caked in mud.

The day was passing fast. I was beginning to feel despair and dread. Maybe my bones were mistaken once again. Then I found a large snakestone, a giant of a serpent, fully two hand spans across! I whooped with delight as I cleaned off the worst of the mud as best I could. A bigwig might pay a golden guinea for one so large.

Joseph seemed to be ignoring my triumph, no doubt because he had only a heap of Devil's fingers and such to show for his efforts. I stood up to see what he was doing. He was staring at something grey, gleaming in the mud.

I felt my heart leap and a pang of jealousy at the same time. I knew in a flash. He had found something very, very special. I knew it even before we washed away the mud with sea water cupped in our frozen hands. It was getting dark as we slowly, carefully, levered off a slice of slate to reveal the great, bony head of a monster.

A monster with a huge round socket in its massive skull and what looked like a saucer cracked all around its rim where its eye had once been. A monster with long, pointed jaws, filled with teeth like tiny daggers. I thought back to my eel skull. It was one tenth the size of this creature!

Joseph tried to lift the slab of rock which was its bed, but it was too heavy, even for him.

'Well, bless my soul!' he marvelled. 'If this is not worth a pretty penny, I'll eat my hat! I must say, Mary, your bones were right again, seemingly, for though I found it, it was you who knew it would be here! This will mark a turn in our fortunes, for sure!'

I wasn't really listening. All the Marys in my head were busy thinking and thinking and looking up at the cliff above and the hole left by the landfall. How had it got so high up? Where had the land been once if such a creature could be in it? Where was the body? This was not a beast beheaded by a fisherman, its body fallen into the sea. This was a giant. A crocodile, most likely.

I thought about some of the ideas Mr Hutton had. From what I could understand, he thought that new rocks were being made all the time deep under the ocean, and then the volcanoes spewed up the rock and covered up what was there before. Was that where the monster had lived, in the land that was now above me before the sea started to wash it away? I supposed that was no different from walking on a path to the beach where once there had been a cottage. The sea devoured the land. I knew that. I saw it every winter. But if Mr Hutton was right, why wasn't more land being made now? More alarming, though, was that he was saying something that would drive church folk wild with rage – that the Earth was not made perfectly in one go as it says in the Bible, in Genesis. It was being made all the time. Was there a volcano in the bay? Would we one day be buried in new rock, waiting to be uncovered? It was a thought that thrilled me but it was a thought I could never dare speak out loud.

I became dimly aware of a voice from outside my head and then Joseph was tapping my shoulder.

'Hey, Mary! You aren't listening to me!'

'I have to find the rest of it,' I said, ignoring him and beginning to pick away at the rock with my hammer and fingers.

'You never will! Be satisfied with what we have found! It's worth good money!'

'The whole skeleton would be worth more,' I replied. I could feel a stubbornness growing inside me. Who was he to tell me what I could or could not do? Had I not known there was something extraordinary in that slab?

I think I would have stayed out all night to guard that mound of mud and rock with its hidden treasure if Joseph had not dragged me to my feet and ordered me home.

'You cannot search any longer, Mary! Be content to return tomorrow. What can you do in the dark?'

I took one last long look at the creature and made a silent promise. 'I will find your body. I will. If it is the last thing I do.'

As we got closer to the house, I tugged on Joseph's jacket to stop him.

'Don't say a word to Mother. Promise me!'

Joseph was confused. 'Why ever not? We have found something quite wondrous and I mean to tell her! Aha! I see how it is! I suppose you are going to sulk after all because it was not *you* who found it!'

I shook my head. 'No, no it is not that. I must find the rest of the creature. Its body! It must be huge if its head is any guide! It will be worth more, much, much more. Please. Do not tell her yet. Let us wait until we have the whole beast. She will want to sell your piece and then the discovery will be wasted!'

'You tell her that if you wish. I want to tell her about the monster! After all, the head is the best bit!'

Mother was amazed and Joseph was proud as a peacock. He seemed to have forgotten all his kind words about me knowing where to look. On and on he went about it being the best find ever and worth a fortune and how it had just fallen at his feet, near enough.

I sat in silence, ate almost nothing and went straight to my bed of rags where I lay awake, listening for the rain, worrying that the slab might all be washed away. I realised I had quite forgotten my giant snakestone. I had been so proud of it, but how small and insignificant it seemed compared to Joseph's find.

I must have fallen asleep for I dreamed strange dreams of gigantic eels with pointed noses and sharp, sharp teeth and when I awoke, I was more determined than ever to find the whole creature and nothing, not even the worst weather, would stop me.

18
WOULD IT PAY TO
BE PATIENT?

*J*oseph was back at work so he had no choice but to entrust me with digging the skull out of the rock. He made a very great fuss in front of Mother about allowing me to 'share in the glory' and how kind he was being letting me take over after he had shown me where to look. Piffle! The fact was that I knew where to look myself and he was too lazy to do the extraction work himself and it didn't interest him in the least in any event. Not that I was unhappy, mind. It suited me down to the ground.

For the first time in her life, Mother wanted to come out with me onto Black Ven. It was not what I wanted at all but she would not take no for an answer. I walked ahead of her as fast as I could, ignoring her calls to slow down or to help her when the ground was difficult to cross.

To be fair, Mother was struck dumb at the sight of the monster. She ran a finger round the eye socket and poked at the teeth. Then, before I knew what she was doing, she took a chisel out of her apron and began trying to extract the beast from its prison of rock, as I suppose she must have seen Father do some time in days gone by. I watched her for a minute or two and then I could stand it no longer.

'No!' I growled, snatching the chisel from her. 'You'll smash the bone or split the rock! Leave it. It will take weeks to do it properly. Father took nearly a month to free a big snakestone and he knew what he was doing. You do not!'

'You mind your manners, young woman!' Mother was in a fury, but I did not care for I was in a bigger fury than she, not least because I was torn in two. I wanted to start my search for the rest of the body, but it was clear that Mother could not be trusted to be left alone with the head.

'Well, do not ruin the best treasure that we have ever found, then!' I retorted. 'Leave me be. I know what I am doing!'

She put her face close to mine. 'We need the money this could fetch, Mary. Surely I do not have to remind you? And do not forget, either, that this could keep you out of a scullery.' Her tone was threatening, but all it did was irritate me more. She'd seen the monster. Now why didn't she just go?

'I know that, thank you, but I will wager that a whole monster is worth a good deal more than part of a monster. Besides, you will get nothing for it before Easter.'

'There's no arguing with you, Mary, is there? You always know best, seemingly!' She dusted her hands violently on her skirt. 'Well, I suppose there is no harm in waiting since, as you say, there'll be no buyers this month or next. You, or rather Joseph' – at this, I pulled a face. I could not help it – 'found it quickly enough. So I am sure the rest will follow in short order. Just remember, time is passing.'

And with that, she turned and set off for home. Good riddance! This was *my* domain, not hers. Mine and Father's.

I suddenly felt very alone. As a rule, I like to be alone. I was glad that Joseph was not with me, not because I did not want him to find any further pieces of the monster . . . well, maybe a bit because of that . . . but because I could concentrate without distraction. Yet under the dark grey sky, in the cutting wind, on the beach beside all the mud and rubble, I felt utterly alone.

A pain shot through my chest. Father! I wanted my father. I wanted him to be there, to tell me what to do next, to protect me and, yes, to praise me and encourage me. After all, I was only here because of him. If he had made me bide at home with Mother when I was a young child, I might have been sewing or cooking now. I might have been looking after the babies. I laughed to myself at this notion. I knew well enough that that would never have happened. One way or another, I would have been here, Father or no Father.

But could I really do this all alone?

I did not like this feeling of doubt. I had never felt I could not do something. I always, always believed I could. Mother called that being stubborn. Father said it was just me being his little Lightning Mary. Where was my lightning now?

I sat on one of the slabs and took the book out of my bag. Why it was called 'Illustrations' I could not fathom, because there weren't any, only hundreds and thousands of difficult words. It seemed the book was about another book which had been so difficult for anyone to understand that Mr Playfair had tried to make it simpler. It was far from simple to me and I doubted I should ever read it all, but I realised that it was enough just to have it with me. It was a scientific work and I was a scientist. Henry believed that. I must believe that. I put it back in my bag.

The creature must have died where it lay for its jaws were complete. By rights, the whole skeleton should be close by. I'd found a rat last winter, frozen to death in the snow, and had hidden it in the graveyard on an untended grave so that I could observe how long it took to turn into a skeleton.

It took much longer than I expected. No other creature seemed to want to eat it and it only really began to decay when the weather got warmer and the flies and maggots came. The skeleton was not picked clean until July. The jaw fell off and all the little bones separated, but it still looked just like a rat. Its teeth and claws and tail were almost the same as in life and even though birds and mice and other rats came and went, it had not been moved. I remembered that Mrs Stock had told me that her cat (the nasty Zebediah) bit the heads off mice, ate all of the body except the stomach and crunched up their little bones as if they were no more than blades of grass. Mrs Stock would come down in the morning to find a head in the scullery, feet in the kitchen and a tiny, nasty, green stomach in the hall.

The monster, the crocodile, had been dead for much, much longer than my rat or any of Zebediah's mice. I could only hope that it had not been killed by something in the way Zebediah killed his prey, or who knows where the bones might be scattered. I shivered to think how big a beast would have to be to behead mine. Zebediah was five times the size of a mouse! No use in imagining that monster, though. I had to concentrate on the job in front of me and hope that the body was close by. I needed something to prove that there would be more to find.

I started work on the slab where Joseph had found the head, painstakingly scraping at the mud and rock, chiselling in to lever off the slices. It was slow progress. How had Joseph been so lucky? He had barely had to work at all!

My hands were beginning to numb, but I worked on until I could no longer hold my tools, then I used my fingers, gritting my teeth at the pain as my nails broke and one even tore off. It must be here! It must! Otherwise . . .

The cliff seemed to lean towards me, blotting out the light. The sea was dark and restless, the tide creeping in.

I just needed a sign that I was looking in the right place, but no. All I found was mud, shale, oyster and mussel shells, roots from a tree torn down long ago.

I was exhausted and my hands were bleeding and filthy. I dabbled them in the shallows and felt the salty water sting my fingertips and sear into the flesh where the nail had been. 'Be brave, Mary,' I told myself. 'It will all be worthwhile in the end.'

I decided to make one last attempt before setting off for home and the explanation that must be made for my failure.

I tugged a section of slab loose and struck it hard along a seam. It fell in two.

At first it seemed there was nothing – but then I saw it. A dull little piece of grey matter. I thought at first that it might be a tooth but when I pulled it out, it was something very different. A round bone, like an apple with the middle spooned out with three pieces coming off one side of it – two like a stubby wing and one pointing straight up like a fin with a hole through the point where they joined. My back ached as I stood up and I rubbed the nape of my neck. My fingers ran over the nobbled bone and I smiled. The head had been attached when it died, for here was the start of its neck.

Where there was a head and a neck, a body should soon follow. There was one difficulty, though. The unexamined slab was no more than a foot long. It was impossible that it contained the whole creature. That meant only one thing.

I looked up at the cliff. It was going to be very difficult to get to the place whence the landfall had come. Difficult and dangerous. The slide had created an overhang but it was that overhang which almost certainly shielded the rest of the beast. How to reach it? If I worked under it and it came loose, I would be crushed. If I worked above it, it would surely collapse even under my small weight and I would fall twenty or thirty feet. Such a fall would most likely maim me. Or kill me.

Well. That was a problem for tomorrow. I had one final task before the sun sank too low.

I had tucked my last piece of paper into the pages of the geology book. I laid the neck bone next to the head and began to make a careful drawing, just as Henry had shown me. Then I wrote '*Skull of a monstrous crocodile found by Joseph Anning under my instruction and verteberry found by me. Sorry about the blood*', folded it up neatly and addressed it to Henry. I put the neck bone in my bag and headed for the town.

'Your brother is going with Nathaniel to fetch the monster,' Mother told me when I got home. 'We cannot risk anyone else finding it. Besides, if it is to take you so long to make it ready for sale, it's better that you do so here. And, no, Mary, I won't touch it! You have made it perfectly plain that I am not as skilled as you.'

Joseph and his friend Nathaniel must have had quite some labours to fetch it from the cliff, for they were red in the face and sweating when they arrived at Cockmoile Square with Nathaniel's wheelbarrow groaning under its load. It took all four of us to manhandle it up the steps into the house where we set it down in the middle of the kitchen floor.

That night, Mother gave us a bit of tallow so that we could have some light as we started the long task of removing all the stone from around the skull and she gave it to us so willingly that I understood her reasoning only too well. I made heavy weather of the task, for the longer I could delay the selling of the skull, the more chance I had of finding the rest of the creature in the cliff.

Mother was not so easily fooled. 'Seems to me, Mary, that you are in no great haste to free that beast,' she remarked, one eyebrow raised.

'I have my reasons,' I replied stoutly. 'See this?' I showed her the neck bone.

'That does not look much like a treasure to me,' she said, turning it over to examine it.

'That, Mother, is proof that the rest of the body is there and I mean to find it. I must find it. You must be patient.'

And I must fathom out a way to find it even though it was in a place I could barely see, much less reach. I could not tell her that.

19

Nothing is Impossible

I returned to 'Joseph's' slab and found nine more verteberries, and then eight great curved rib bones, thin as a whip, curved at the top. I thought of the horse and how its ribs bowed out to protect its heart and lungs. I felt the length of my own ribs, an easy task as I had little meat on my bones. The creature must have been two or three times as broad as me.

I drew each piece as faithfully as I could and numbered them so I could remember the order in which I had found each item. Much to my pleasure, Henry wrote that I was nearly as good as he at a likeness! I am not one for flattery, but I was pleased by his good opinion of my drawing, which was much improved through practice.

I had also found some curious strands of bone and little square pieces like tiles. At first, I thought they might be broken pieces of a larger bone but they were so well-formed and rounded that they must surely have some purpose of their own. It was like having very few pieces of a puzzle.

There weren't enough to be able to guess what the finished picture would be like. Only when I had the whole creature could I really solve the puzzle. I needed a miracle but a miracle would not come for the asking, it seemed.

I spent many hours staring up at the cliff, willing it to come crashing down at my feet, but it was as stubborn as I was and remained unmoved, unchanged. I started praying for rain, for storms, but none came. There was nothing to be done, it seemed, and that made me boil with frustration. I persuaded Mother to let me keep the skull a while longer, at least until my birthday in May, but that came and went and I felt I would have nothing to celebrate until the whole cliff collapsed.

Reluctantly I returned to my 'bread and butter' work, for I had to make sure we had enough curiosities to sell to the visitors. We also sold snakestones to farmers, only they called them crampstones. They used them to treat beasts with the colic by soaking the stones in water and then giving the water to the beast to drink. Some folk believed a snakestone could cure a snakebite but Mrs Stock said that was nonsense and she'd heard tell of a shepherd who got bitten by an adder when out on the heath and was found all swollen up like a cow with bloat and a snakestone clutched in his dead hand and it hadn't saved him. Still, people will pay good money for them and it is not any of my business if they choose to believe

194

nonsense. I make no such promises. Nor do I paint serpent heads or eyes on the stones to trick people, as some do.

Mother seemed to have forgotten how I had berated her for her clumsy attempts with a chisel and came out with me on these expeditions all through that long spring. At first I could not abide to have her near me. I showed her what to look for and left her to it. It was strange to have her call to me to come and praise her for some small thing she had found and I could not pretend to be impressed when she showed me her pitiful pile of fish bones. In the end, I told her to confine herself to finding pretty shells since there were always ladies who took a fancy to those. Mother was happy enough to do so and it meant that I was free from her eternally asking me whether she had found part of the monster or something rare when all she had was some odd-shaped stone or a bit of sea glass. She did one day tap a rock and reveal a very fine snakestone, but she was so noisy in her celebration that I prayed heartily that she would never find one again.

We were a force to be reckoned with when it came to selling, though, and there was no mistake that two women were better at getting money out of a customer than any man. Maybe I did get my trading skills from her, for Mother was a demon for driving a hard bargain. Sometimes I think folk came to our table of treasures just to gawp at Mother and me. It was a shame we could not charge them to stare at us. We would have cleared our debts the faster.

Most of our customers were just looking for some cheap keepsake from their holiday, but one visitor to our stall was different. She spent some time examining each piece and she seemed to know which the most interesting specimens were.

I found myself staring at her and then I remembered where I had seen her. She had bought that ram's horn from me, more than two years back, in the graveyard. She stared at me too and smiled.

'I see you remember me, Miss Anning. Do you know what you started that day you sold me the ammonite?'

'Ram's horn,' I corrected. Lord knows what an ammonite was. 'What did I start?'

'A collection. I have followed in your footsteps. Not literally, I hasten to add, for I am not so intrepid a collector as you, but I have found, and purchased, some treasures. You may care to come and see them?' She held out a gloved hand. 'I'm Elizabeth Philpot and—'

'Ha! The same Philpots as make Philpot's Salve?' interrupted Mother. 'You must make a pretty penny from that.'

Miss Philpot smiled again. 'The very same. Have you ever used it, Mrs Anning?'

Mother snorted. 'Not I! There's no money for fancy ointments for the likes of us!'

'I *would* like to see what you have got,' I said, before Mother could waste any more time talking about ointment. 'Now. If you please.'

She nodded her assent and before Mother could complain, we set off to climb the hill to her house – a long, low, rambling building with a thatch and painted the same pink as a boiled crab.

She took me into a room lined from floor to ceiling with books and there, in the centre, stood a great wooden case with a glass lid. She took a key from a drawer in the desk and opened the case.

'Come. Please. Examine the pieces, if you wish. You will see that your "ram's horn" is in pride of place.'

She had quite an assembly of treasures: delicate fish skeletons sunk into slate, a starfish, one of the best scuttles I had ever seen and a number of very good snakestones and rams' horns, of which mine was, I had to say, quite clearly the best.

'I've never seen you on the beach and you did not buy all of these from us. How did you come by them?' I asked.

'Oh, I found most of them myself. I am a fair weather treasure-hunter, though, it's true. Not out in all weathers like you. Perhaps I might accompany you one day? Would you consider that? I know I would like it very much!'

'Well, I wouldn't. What name did you give my ram's horn?'

'It's a type of ammonite. Named for the Greek ram-headed god, Ammon, so you were on the right lines. It's the name collectors give them, scientific collectors. I could lend you a book, if you like. Or several. On the science behind these creatures. This is a favourite of mine.' She held out a slim volume.

'I've got a book on geology already,' I said. 'But there are no pictures. Does this one have pictures?'

She looked shamefaced. 'Of course! How foolish of me! I could teach you to read, though, then you could profit from this library!'

'I can read perfectly well, thank you very much. Just because we are poor does not mean we are stupid. I just wish to see proper illustrations, correctly labelled so that I may compare my finds and observations more readily.' I took the book from her, a little roughly I must admit.

'Oh dear! We have got off on the wrong foot. Please forgive me. I hoped we might be friends!'

'I've got a friend,' I said. 'He's away being a soldier but he will come back and be a scientist with me soon enough.'

It was good to be able to tell her about being a scientist but I rather hoped she did not think she was one herself.

'It's lovely that you have a friend,' she responded, smiling all the while. 'I am happy for you, Mary, but might you not have time for another friend in the meantime? I promise not to inconvenience you or irritate you. You can borrow my books and perhaps we could visit the beach together? Oh, and I can introduce you to some people who would be very interested to meet you and might help you in your endeavours?'

I studied her face for a moment. She seemed sincere. Maybe I had been too hasty.

'You know, Mary, I get a tingling feeling when I find a creature in the rocks. To think that it might have lived untold years ago! It is quite a thought, isn't it? It makes me feel so insignificant! We are here such a short time. How do we make our mark? Do I want to be known only for a salve? Or do I want to leave some legacy behind me that means I will be remembered for ever? I think you know that feeling, Mary, even though you are so young. I think you are like me. On a quest. A quest for truth and knowledge. I am not interested in trinkets or gewgaws or baubles. I want to have a collection as good as any in London, and why shouldn't I? What is to stop us, Mary, from doing whatever we wish?'

I was struck by her mention of 'untold years'! Did she mean she shared Mr Hutton's ideas? She had not hesitated to speak those words so she did not seem at all afraid of my reaction. It would be good to be able to discuss such things with one as bold as she and to do so in safety.

And maybe we were alike, I thought, even though she was

older and richer and more learned. I wondered if I should tell her about the monster but I bit my tongue. It was too soon to give her so much trust, and yet I felt deep in my bones that I might like her before too long and maybe she could help me understand more about geology.

I held her gaze for a moment and, thanking her for the book, added, 'I shall be seeking shells on the seashore this evening. We could go together if you wish?'

'I do wish!' she replied, clapping her hands. 'I do indeed!'

Miss Philpot and I spent many evenings hunting for shells and she was a pleasant and knowledgeable companion. She knew the scientific names for things that I found and soon I knew them all too, and that was very useful. At first, I did not ask her outright what she thought about God and the Creation but I felt I might soon trust her enough to do so and, sure enough, within a few days we were discussing all manner of ideas and notions.

One day, as we walked up Silver Street to her house for tea, Elizabeth (as I now called her) stopped by the forge and together we watched as the horseshoes were heated red hot in the furnace, hammered into shape on the forge and plunged into buckets of water, which boiled and hissed like a wild creature.

'What do you think, Mary?' she asked. 'Was the Earth

forged in volcanic fire or dissolved in the oceans? Are you a Plutonist or a Neptunist?'

How glad I was that I had battled with the book Mrs Stock had given me and knew a little of these matters.

'Mr Hutton and Mr Playfair have influenced me to feel more inclined to fire than water as the force behind the Earth, even though I dwell by the sea and observe her workings daily. She seems more to take away land than to build it up. I like to think of the rock as the pages of a great book and the creatures trapped inside like pressed flowers and that means new rock on top of old,' I said, rather proud to be naming such gentlemen and proving my understanding of their work.

Elizabeth smiled and looked, dare I say it, rather proud of me herself.

Even as I voiced these thoughts, I found the Marys in my head getting in a frightful state of confusion. One Mary wanted to shut her ears to any talk that did not agree with the Holy Book, for I knew that most folk would say that it was neither the fire nor the sea that formed the Earth but only the work of God the Almighty, Creator of all this world and every creature in it. Another could only think that the six days of Creation were but a story and agree with my father that if they were days, they were very much longer ones than we had now. Very much longer.

It seemed Elizabeth could read my mind for she replied,

'That book analogy of yours is a very good one. I wonder how many tens of thousands of years might have passed in the laying down and wearing away of each page of rock. More than we can imagine, no doubt. And what creatures might be caught up in its leaves, stranger even than the ones in my cabinets?'

It was a thought that had occurred to me in almost every waking hour. I had even wondered if creatures like the monster might have been mistakes that God had then deliberately destroyed and buried, but then I shrank back from the idea in fear and horror. Could God make mistakes? It was not something that could be said out loud. Or was it?

Elizabeth's eyes met mine. She looked at me as if she knew all about the battles the Marys fought in my head, and expected one of them to say something bold or shocking.

'You'll find those creatures, Mary. Of that, I am sure,' she said when I remained silent.

That was a moment to tell her about the monster but I did not. I was not ready. I did not have enough to tell her. It was enough for now to think how I might progress and learn through discussion.

Another thing greatly in Elizabeth's favour was that she did not irritate me. Maybe it was no accident that her family had made their fortune from a salve that could soothe a burn or heal a cut, for she was calm and soothing herself.

Not that she would have been able to calm my secret

torment at the thought of that monster body still out there, beyond my reach. I lay awake night after night, trying to solve the problem of how to find it.

I had tried to climb up the cliff face but I could not get close enough, and it was impossible to get a proper grip anywhere. I managed to clamber up about fifteen feet, but the slab with the skull in it had come from even higher, another ten feet or more, and above that was the overhang created by the landslip. Imagine looking up to a roof of mud and roots and rock that you know could fall on you at any moment. It is a far from pleasant prospect.

One day, I went into the field above the cliff and looked over the edge to see if I could get any closer that way. The overhang wasn't part of the headland, as I had assumed, but ten feet lower. It must have already started to slip and got stuck. That meant it was very unstable indeed.

I have never minded climbing up things, but even I am wary of going down. I could hear Father's voice in my head, warning me of the treachery of Black Ven, of all the lives lost – man and beast – but I had to be brave, had to try.

I very carefully lowered myself onto a ledge above the overhang, but even as my feet touched the earth, it was clear that my weight was too great. A wave of terror went through me and, even as the shower of rocks went tumbling down,

I managed to scramble back over the lip of the cliff and onto the grass by the very skin of my teeth. I lay on my belly with my cheek pressed to the earth and my heart racing, all the while trying to fathom a method by which I might get to that body.

I lay there a while. The ground was cold and damp. All was silent, save for the sea's back and forth on the beach fifty feet below. I wondered what would have happened if I had lost my footing. How had Father felt that day he had his accident? Had he grasped at the mud and rock in desperation as he fell? Had he thought he was sure to die?

Then I fell to wondering if I was even alive now? Maybe I *had* fallen to my death? Maybe I was dead already? How could I tell if this was real or a dream or even the life to come? I must confess that I frightened myself with these thoughts for they were not sensible or scientific. Yet, somehow, I passed several minutes wondering how I might prove to myself that I was still alive. Maybe it was because I had had a glimpse of death.

Suddenly I felt warm breath on the back of my head and turned over to come face to face with a cow. A long skein of drool landed on my face as she jerked her head back in fear. I wiped it away with my sleeve and sat up. The cow had been joined by several others, though they were less brave or less curious than she, for they stood back in a huddle, jostling each other gently and snorting clouds of steam.

'I must be alive then,' I said aloud, as the cows all retreated backwards, their gaze still fixed on me.

I stood up and they all turned and fled, two bucking like horses, the rest skittish and silly. I had been their adventure for the day. The cliff had been mine. An adventure I was in no hurry to repeat.

One thing was clear. I needed another landslip. But that was in the hands of Nature and the weather. It might take months, years. How could I wait that long? How could I ensure Mother would wait that long?

I needed to think. Instead of going home, I walked through the fields towards Rhode Barton so that I should come back down into town round the back of Squire Stock's farm, a walk of three miles or more. Enough time to clear my mind and make space for new ideas.

As I climbed Dragon Hill (how well-named it would prove!), I saw there was some commotion up ahead at a sharp bend in the cart track. A group of men were hammering stakes into the bank above the woods, watched by quite a crowd. I recognised one of them as Josiah Jenkins, quarryman.

I ran up to look over the edge. A carriage and two horses lay at the bottom of the slope, some thirty feet down. The horses were thrashing about, trying to get up, but pinned to the ground by their traces. The carriage had lost two of its wheels. The coachman was standing up but holding his shoulder and moaning. He had blood on his head and clothes. I could not see any passengers.

An old woman came to stand by me, yellowed eyes bright with excitement. She took a hold of my arm with her clawed fingers but seemed not to mind when I shook her off.

'Two people in that carriage. Dead, I expect. One of they horses be mortally wounded, for certain sure. No one can get up and no one can get down, for tis slippery as an eel's back and that carriage be wedged in the goyle and it isn't goin' to move so easy. There's a poor body underneath, see. Fell out of the windy on the way down and then the 'ole carriage fell on 'e! Tis a pretty pickle and no word of a lie!'

She rubbed her hands in glee at the spectacle but my eyes were fixed elsewhere.

More men had arrived with ropes. They lashed them to the stakes. Two of the men then began to climb down backwards, the rope looped around their waists, their feet against the steep bank. They slowly paid out the rope as they almost bounced down the side of the hill. It was wondrous clever!

That was when it came to me. There was a way that Black Ven could be made to yield its treasure!

'In't you goin' to see 'em saved?' shouted the old woman as I set off back down the hill.

But I had no interest in saving anything but that monster in the mud! Nothing is impossible, I told myself. Nothing!

20

BONES FROM STONES

I found Josiah Jenkins again in the tavern the next day. He was busy telling a small crowd how he had rescued the people from the goyle, hoisting up the fellow who had been crushed, laid out on an old door.

'Wasted our time with that one,' he said, taking another great gulp from a tankard. 'Died not two hours later on account of him being squashed like a tomato. Had to shoot a horse with my pistol too. Poor beast. Broken its back and shoulder, I reckon. The other one was sound as a pound. Landed on his fellow, see, like a cushion.'

He suddenly noticed me standing close by.

'Ah! I seen you up at the accident, but you ran off. Was you afear'd?'

'Me! Afear'd? Not in the least. I am here because I have a commission for you.'

He laughed and I did not much like the way of it. I stood up tall. Sometimes, even though it is a very great bother to be a woman, it can serve me well for I do not feel like a girl child speaking to a man, but another growed-up personage, equal to equal.

'There's coin in it, if you do the job to my standards!' I said stoutly, for I wasn't going to have any nonsense from him.

One of his drinking companions leaned towards him and whispered in the loudest whisper ever heard: 'Tis Richard Anning's daughter. Him what fell off of Black Ven and took sick and died, and her that little maid what was struck by lightning and lived. She's a little scrapper, that one! You want to be careful!'

'Richard's daughter, eh? I've seen you on the beach, ferreting about, haven't I?' He looked me up and down and I did not much like that, either. 'Well, what is your great commission, then?'

'I need you to help me get to a place on The Spittles. With your ropes and stakes. You must first dislodge a portion of the cliff, which can be easily done for my weight alone was sufficient to loosen it, and then I need you to teach me how I may walk down the cliff face as your men did walk down the slope to the goyle. And you must also help me to transport matter from the cliff back to Lyme.'

'Matter? What matter?'

'Never you mind what matter,' I said. 'Will you do it?'

'It'll be dangerous,' said he, taking a mighty swig from his tankard.

'Not if you set the stakes far from the cliff edge,' I retorted.

He looked at me with respect. 'I meant for you, Miss Anning. I see you have your father's stubborn nature, though, so I suppose danger don't bother you any?'

'It does not. Not when it can be avoided by careful management.'

The men all chortled with laughter at this. I ignored them.

'No doubt you will expect payment in advance but I make you this offer: you may have a guinea now or ten per cent of the' – I nearly said treasure – 'matter, when it is sold. Which requires you to wait. But it will be worth it,' I added.

'Matter, eh? You found silver, Miss Anning? Gold, even?'

'More wondrous treasure than that,' I replied.

'It'll be nothing but an old skellington, you mark my words!' said the man who had called me a scrapper. 'You know how Richard was with his curiosities. Fancy folk do pay good money for 'em, mind. You found something special, missy?'

'I have,' I said, for I was not inclined to tell them more lest they went looking themselves.

Josiah Jenkins pulled on his whiskers and whistled through his few teeth. 'Well, Miss Anning. I liked your father. I quite like your mother.' He winked. I stared at him with my most stony face. 'But mostly, I likes a gamble so you have yourself a deal. Here. Shake on it.'

He spat into the palm of his large hand, its back hairy as a dog's paw, and held it out to me. I spat on mine and then endured his grasp for a moment. It was unpleasant.

'Tomorrow. Up at The Spittles. Seven of the clock.' And with that I left them to their ale and went home, well pleased with my trade and much relieved, for I did not have a single penny in my pocket and I had not been obliged to admit it.

'Let me understand you, Mary,' Mother said as she folded her apron and sat down on our one chair. 'You want to spend money we do not have to find a treasure which may not exist and, even if it does, is in a place which cannot be reached? Have you taken leave of your senses?'

'But it *can* be reached,' I replied. 'With men and ropes. I have a plan. I know it will work.'

'But you do not know that your monster will be found. That you cannot know. T'would be lives risked and money wasted!'

I stood my ground. 'It will be done in safety and will be money well spent.'

'Why you are so fixed on this enterprise, I do not know!' said Mother crossly. 'What does it matter if there is more of the creature in those rocks! We have the head! Those bits and pieces you have found are of no interest to anybody! They look like sticks and pebbles to me, in any event.'

'You wait, Mother. You wait to see what I will find. I tell you now, t'will make us famous. Folk will come from miles around to wonder at it.'

'Folk already do,' retorted Mother sourly. 'I suppose this is more science nonsense put into your head by Miss Lotions and Potions.'

'You mean Miss Philpot,' I muttered under my breath, but Mother continued.

'Or maybe Master La-di-da De la Beach, or that book you hide about your person. Oh yes, missy, I know about your letters and your book!'

'Tis too late, in any event!' I said triumphantly. 'For the plans are in hand and the men instructed.'

This took the wind out of Mother's sails! 'How so?'

'I have pledged them a share of the money I shall make from the sale. Tis all arranged and cannot be undone.'

'Why would growed men take instruction from a twelve-year-old?' she asked, though more in wonderment than wanting an answer to this rather stupid question since she herself well knew that I was famed for my fierceness.

In fact, though, the men were doing it less for my fierceness and more for their own amusement, truth be told. So be it. Their reasons were of little interest to me.

The next morning, I was up on The Spittles early. To my amazement and delight, the overhang had already begun to make its way down the cliff. It would surely not take much to send it on its way.

Suddenly someone grabbed me and pulled me back from the edge. Joseph!

'Followed you. Mother said to. What crazed plan is this?'

'Just you watch,' I said. 'I am going to walk down that cliff as if it were as flat as the shore!'

Just then, Josiah Jenkins came puffing up the hill, hauling ropes and two great stakes, helped by another, a labourer, and I recognised him as one of the men who had descended on the ropes. He said nothing to me or to Joseph. Josiah never said his name and I never asked it.

Josiah peered over the edge. I explained my plan. He shook his head. I stamped my foot. He argued, I argued back.

After much huffing and puffing, they started work and soon had the stakes deep into the turf.

The silent man took a hold of one of the ropes, looped it around his waist and began to walk backwards to the cliff edge, staring straight ahead of him all the while. I admired his courage as he stepped back and over the lip and then disappeared from view. Joseph and I approached carefully. Below us, the man jumped onto the loosened slab and began bouncing on it. Earth and stones began to clatter down the cliff face. Behind us, Josiah braced himself against the stake as it trembled with every blow struck to the cliff by the man on the rope.

All of a sudden there was a great rumbling and the entire slab went crashing down to the beach. The man with no name hauled himself back up again. His face was as blank as a fresh sheet of paper. He rubbed his hands on his smock and I saw that they were red and sore from the roughness of the rope. I looked down at my own. Would I be strong enough to hold on?

'Now you must teach me to go down for I need to search the rock for—'

'For the matter?' Josiah asked, winking at me.

'Yes. The matter.' I glared at Joseph lest he say anything, but he seemed to understand my reason for secrecy.

'Maybe I should go,' he said. 'It's a man's job.'

I ignored him. I picked up the second rope and tried to copy the silent man. He smiled and gently showed me how to arrange the rope.

Josiah tied another rope around my waist. 'I'll have a hold of this. In case,' he said. 'Joseph? I'll keep on this stake. You take the other.'

They leaned back on the stakes, Josiah with the rest of my lifeline coiled beside him, Joseph quite white-faced.

My teacher nodded his head, indicating I should follow him as he started to move backwards to the cliff edge again.

However brave a body may be, it is not a good feeling to walk backwards over a cliff while trying to pay out a rope and hang onto it at the same time. I was more glad of that lifeline than I could say, but even that was not sufficient to overcome my terror. My hands felt slippery with sweat one moment and as if they would not work at all the next. My heart was beating so hard, I feared it would set off a landslip of its own.

I wondered how I could take that first step backwards off the edge. The silent man spoke. He had a calm, quiet voice.

'Look at me. Do as I do. Do not look back. Do not look down. Keep your body like this.' He was braced against the rope and at an angle to the ground, leaning back. 'Ready? You have to give a little jump to be free of the cliff. Just for a moment. You will swing out and back in again. Be ready with your feet.'

Do not ask me how I made that leap. In truth, I did it only because I was fixed on my teacher and as he jumped, so did I. For what seemed like an eternity, I swung out, forty, fifty feet above the shore and then, bang, I was back with my feet against the mud. I felt sick but I also felt a kind of wild joy.

Together, my teacher and I made our way down to the point I sought.

I realised that I was powerless to do anything, both hands being occupied. What if nothing could be seen? What if I needed to dig away the mud? Maybe I could just kick it off?

There was no ledge on which to rest. I could only hang on for dear life, the ropes around my waist cutting into me, my palms already raw. I prayed to God that there would be something to see. Something to prove the monster's presence.

There, sticking out from between the layers, was a slice of stone, dotted with bones, some tile-like, others longer and all fanning out from the end of a much thicker bone, like to the foreleg of a giant hog.

The silent man followed my gaze, but looked confused. 'Is that what you hoped for?' he asked. 'For it looks like no more than stones to me.'

'Not stones,' I said. 'Bones. I think that we have found the creature's hand!'

'It looks like no hand I have ever seen!'

'Like no hand anyone has ever seen!' I cried, anxious to be back up on the cliff top. 'Pull us up!'

'Nay, missus!' smiled the silent man. 'You've to pull yourself up!' And he showed me how it was done.

Clambering back up was harder than going down, even with Josiah pulling on the extra rope, and once again I found myself face down at the top of the cliff, my heart racing, barely believing I had survived. After a few minutes, I got up and undid the ropes.

Joseph was looking at me with pride and curiosity. 'Well? Is it there?' he asked.

'It is! Now,' I turned to Josiah, 'we must devise a way for me to get to it so that I may dig it out!'

21

WHAT MANNER OF CREATURE IS THIS?

*J*osiah made me a sort of platform which was more like a swing, in truth, for it was a thick plank hung from two ropes lashed to new stakes on the cliff top and the slightest movement sent it rocking like a boat on the waves.

Mother walked up the hill but could not bring herself to look over the edge at my device. I had become skilled at getting myself down the cliff face and then onto the plank and it quite amused me to see Mother's face go pale with fear as I leaped backwards over the edge.

'What a creature you are, Mary, to be hanging off a cliff, hunting for monsters. How did I ever birth such a body?' she shouted to me, her voice quavering with worry.

Within a week, Joseph and I had winched up the wedge of stone containing the 'hand' which I soon realised must in reality be the beast's foot or fin. Joseph was not impressed by it at all. He just saw a jumble of bones, but a theory was building in my head and I needed only to find more to be able to prove it. Elizabeth, of course, was as excited as I was and not at all upset that I had not told her of my find before. We gave each other secret looks of glee as the weeks went by and the treasure grew and grew.

I had devised a simple method for getting the smaller pieces back up the cliff. I tied one end of a long rope to one of the stakes and the other to a sack and dropped that over the edge. I could not sketch anything while I was wobbling on the plank so I had to stare at each piece and commit it to memory before dropping it in the sack. I gave Mother the job of hauling it up and emptying it out on the grass but she would not come close enough to the edge to throw it back down again so she was not of much use. Still, she and Joseph took their turn, she by day, he on Saturdays and Sundays between Chapel services and in the evenings after work, waiting on the grass, holding onto my safety rope and checking the stakes to make sure they did not work loose.

The cliff face really was like the pages of a book made of thick vellum and the bones were revealed on a slab like a page pulled out from the binding. It was hard work digging into the rock while the swing moved from side to side. Sometimes I felt quite seasick. I knew I must never look down so I was very careful not to drop anything and, besides, who knows how long it would have taken me to find it again at the bottom of the cliff?

People came to stare at me, some out of curiosity, some out of concern. I would not have been surprised to see the old crone who had had so much pleasure from the coach smash, but perhaps it was too far for her old legs. Two girls came to giggle and squeal. One of them threw me down an apple, which nearly struck me and I made the mistake of watching it bounce down the cliffs, getting smashed to small pieces as it went. It was a waste of an apple and it was a while before I felt composed enough to continue. I could not stop the vision of my father's accident from forming in my head. I told the girls to go away.

'You are very brave, Mary Anning!' one of them shouted over the edge. 'I could not do such a thing!'

Was I brave? I didn't think so. I was quite frightened most of the time, but then Harry May told me that that was what true bravery was – doing something when you were afraid.

Then, one day all was changed. The rain came. It fell in torrents, and for five days I could not get to the cliff – and when I did, nothing remained of my platform save one post, and that was pulled almost out of the ground.

I went as close to the edge as I dared. It was a scene of devastation, my platform gone and with it a goodly chunk of the cliff, but my heart leaped in my chest.

I ran back down the hill and onto the beach as fast as

I could, stumbling in the mud as I scrambled towards the fresh landslip.

There was the rest of the page! A long slab, split to reveal almost as many remnants of the monster as I had already uncovered. Another 'hand', with three long spindly 'fingers' all made up of tiny tiles and a long, long tail, maybe as long as I was tall. My dragon! My monster! If only Father was there, or Henry. I fell onto my knees and felt a storm brew up in my head, all the Marys rushing about. I had never felt so alive or so alone.

I was so proud to tell Mother and Elizabeth that I had succeeded in my goal.

What a mistake it was to tell Mother, though, for she gossiped and word spread like wildfire. The shore became crowded with gawpers. How it amused and irritated me to observe people's disappointed or disgusted faces when they saw the great mounds of bones yet to be assembled. What did they expect? My task had scarce begun!

Joseph, Nathaniel and I barrowed the bones back to Cockmoile Square to stand in muddy heaps, awaiting my attention.

'Don't look like nothing to me!' complained the house-keeper from Colway Manor, the grand home of Lord Henley, but she went back and told His Lordship's manservant and he told his master and next thing we knew a message was sent that His Lordship wished to see the creature and that it must be brought up to him for viewing.

The stupidity of such a request put me in a very bad humour but Mother, of course, was anxious for a sale and sent her 'humble request' that he visit.

He came the very next day.

'Well, the skull is rather fine, I suppose,' His Lordship said languidly, holding a handkerchief over his nose as fancy folk are wont to do, their noses being so very intolerant of anything but their own stink. 'But as for these' – he gestured at the piles with his cane – 'these are of no interest at all! I will take the beast's head, however.'

'You won't and you are wrong, sir,' I said, ignoring Mother's look of horror. 'And ignorant, I daresay.'

Mother had gone quite white, His Lordship quite silent.

'But that is not your fault, for you can never have seen such a creature before,' I added, for it seemed he must somehow be excused. 'And if you return a month from now, you will see how wrong you were. Now, if you please, I have a great deal of work to do!'

Mother, now red-faced, led him away. It was to be hoped that he had more ready money in his pocket than he had brains in his skull.

I had persuaded Joseph and Nathaniel to move the beast to Father's old workshop, which was empty, and there

I began to lay it out so that it might be seen whole. Miss Philpot was away in London, or I would have had her help me.

How did I know where each piece belonged in a creature no one had ever seen? I had observed and rebuilt a great many skeletons, just as Mr De Luc had advised me to do when I saw that dead horse, and when I had studied my precious eel skull which still sits by my bed. Putting a creature together seems to me as natural as breathing.

Joseph had built me a shallow bed for the creature, a bit like a tray, which I filled with clay into which I could press the bones, sprinkling water in the clay from time to time to keep it damp and covering it with a damp cloth by night. Little by little, day by day, the creature's body grew back from its great head, the long arched spine, the huge ribcage all took shape. As I placed each piece, joined each vertebra (which was the proper name for them, Elizabeth said), it was as if I could feel the creature twist and turn beneath my touch. The 'hands' still confused me. I laid them out as I had found them and suddenly I could see quite clearly what they were because they reminded me of an oar held in place by the rollock, the blade beating back the water. My monster swam in the sea, his great fins like paddles, sending him through the water with the ease of a bird flying in the sky. I could see these pictures in my head as clearly as if they were real, but I could not easily explain them to anybody else except Elizabeth.

I worked away on my own and in silence until one afternoon, when I was interrupted.

'That is quite some monster you have there! May I come and look?'

A figure stood in the doorway, blocking out the light. For a moment, I thought it was Henry, but this was someone older and taller.

'If you must,' I said, but he was already in, dancing round the bones, twiddling his hat and whooping with excitement.

'Oh my word! What a specimen! What a find! What a clever thing you are! Remarkable! Remarkable! Oh, my dear! This is quite stupendous!'

'Will you stop with your jigging, sir,' I said and I was quite cross because he danced so close that one false move might send bones flying, undoing weeks of work.

'What? Yes, of course! Look at that head! That magnificent head! That eye! Can you imagine that eye, rolling in that socket, seeking out its prey, hunting in the gloomy depths! And those teeth! What a creature! What a creature!'

He paused for breath and held out his hand.

'Buckland. William. Fellow, Corpus Christi. Mineralogist! Friend of Miss Elizabeth Philpot. Heard all about you! Heard about your creature. Had to come straightaway and see it for myself! Magnificent! So, what's your theory, ma'am? What is this beast, d'you think?' The mad fellow of Corpus Christi, whoever or whatever that might be, was hopping from one leg to another in his excitement.

'Lord Henley says he is a giant crocodile,' I replied cautiously.

'Ah, but *you* do not think that, do you? I see by your face that you do not! What do you think? He's not a crocodile. Seen plenty of those. He's not a fish. He's not a lizard. What's this fellow's name, eh? Shall we give him a name? Fish Lizard? Would that do?'

'Fish Lizard is not a very scientific name,' I countered, almost lost for words.

'It's not. It's not, dear lady, you are quite right. We must give him a proper name, shall we? Ichthyosaurus. *Ichthyosaur. Ichthy*, fish and *saurus*, lizard. Sound about right to you? Of course I will have to discuss it with my scientific colleagues before we settle on such a title but it will do for now. What a beast! Would not want to meet *that* whilst you were taking the waters, would you? By Jove, no!'

'Do you want to buy it?' I asked, for I was beginning to tire of all his noise and hopping about.

'How I wish I could! How I very much wish I could! No money, dear lady!' He pulled his pockets inside out to prove it. 'We scholars live on short rations, I can tell you! Must you sell it? I suppose you must. On short rations yourself, I shouldn't wonder. Take care you get a fair price. There are fellows who would take advantage of a lady.'

'They will not easily take advantage of me,' I said, showing him the door, for I was quite exhausted.

'Indeed not! Indeed not! I will leave you to your labours. What patience! This is the work of many months, I can see that! What an achievement! A remarkable find, dear lady. Remarkable! An honour to meet you. Heard so much. Your fame. Spreading. Remarkable! So young! So wise! Remarkable! William Buckland. At your service!'

And with a last 'remarkable' which seemed to be his favourite word, he finally disappeared.

Elizabeth was most amused when I told her of his visit and imitated him rushing about and talking nineteen to the dozen. 'He's worth knowing, Mary,' she informed me. 'He is well respected for his academic work and has the very best connections in our field of interest, though I grant he is a very eccentric fellow!'

Eccentric? Quite deranged, if you ask me!

I told Henry about him too, and it seemed Elizabeth was right, for Henry wrote back to say that he was envious of me spending my time in the company of such illustrious folk as William Buckland while he was forced to play at soldiers and fall off his horse at regular intervals.

'*You'll be more of an expert geologist than I'll ever be, at this rate,*' he wrote. '*But what a pity that you must sell the creature, the Fish Lizard! I can only hope it makes your fortune!*'

My fortune? What would Lord Henley of Colway Manor pay for a Fish Lizard?

Not a fortune, it seemed.

'Twenty-five pounds. Take it or leave it.' Lord Henley had sent his estate manager to pay for the creature. A stony-faced, stony-hearted man, evidently quite set on carrying out his orders to the letter and giving no ground.

'Is Lord Henley going to keep it? Is he going to keep it or sell it on?' I demanded, for I knew of folk who had bought curiosities from me for pennies and sold them to their rich friends for pounds, something which made me very angry indeed.

'It is of no business to you what His Lordship chooses to do with his possessions, and since the beast was found on his land he is being more than generous in paying you at all!'

'That's as may be, but he did not have the talent to find it, the skill or patience to dig it out *or* the sense to see what a creature it was!' said I.

The manager's face changed not one jot. 'You'll not get a better offer. In point of fact, you'll not *get* another offer.'

He cast a disdainful gaze around our kitchen, noting the empty shelves, the one chair. I felt my anger rising but, before

I could stop her, Mother had said 'Done' and stuffed the little bag of coins in her pinny.

And that was that. Gone in a trice.

I did not help them as they loaded my monster in his bed of clay into a crate and onto the cart. The crate looked like a coffin to me. A coffin for a giant. That creature had been my life for more than a year and now it was gone, leaving me only the drawings in my sketchbook and a pain in my heart.

I went round to the alehouse to pay Josiah, but he would not take the money. He said I was the bravest little maid he had ever met and it had been a pleasure to be of assistance. How surprising people are! There seems no way to tell for certain from their outside whether they'll be nice or nasty.

I felt quite lost for many days after. I had no energy for anything, no inclination to go searching, even though Elizabeth told me over and over again that if there was one monster out there, there would be others.

The truth was that I missed the excuse to spend day after day in Father's workshop. Even though not so much a splinter of wood or a speck of sawdust remained, I could still feel close to him somehow. The monster had taken his place in my life and then it had brought me close to him again and now it was gone and he was gone.

Lord Henley sold my monster on, of course. William Buckland told Elizabeth and she could not keep it secret from me because she was so outraged on my behalf. William Bullock's Museum of Natural Curiosities paid one hundred pounds, so it was said, but that might have been a falsehood. It was Joseph's name that went on the cabinet when it was displayed and I suppose he did find the skull, but only because I knew where to look.

There was no use moaning about it. Some days it made me angry. Some days I did not care at all. Mostly, it made me grit my teeth, determined to show them what I, Lightning Mary, could do, woman or not. But there were days, dark days, when I felt as if I had lined up for a race and then been told to take two steps back because I was poor, and then two steps back because Father had been a Dissenter, and then *ten* steps back because I was not a man. Yet, for all that, I could still beat them.

Only thing was, even when I won, they would not give me the prize.

22
REMEMBRANCE AND REUNION

*T*hat monster, that extraordinary find, sometimes felt as if it had been the start of my life and the end of it. I have never paid much attention to people's opinion of me, for what do opinions matter? They cannot change a body or that is what I have always believed. It is hard, though, to be unaffected by the talk and I see how it hardened me and made me both more determined and more clear-sighted about how people use other people for their own ends.

For some, I was a prodigy to be admired. For others, I was dismissed as an oddity, a curiosity to be gawped at and prodded like the two-headed calf paraded at the fair in Uplyme. Few thought there was skill in my find, only luck . . . and that luck down to Joseph's discovery. They could not know what pains I had taken and they were not interested enough to find out.

There was an expectation that I would find more. It was an expectation I had of myself too. And it was an expectation

Mother had, for she had acquired a taste for the fame – and for the money to be made from a large find.

Fame brought me other attention that I neither welcomed nor relished. Seems it was my fate to be the subject of a childish rhyme once again, often chanted by children as I made my way across the beach. 'She sells sea shells on the seashore' was, I must own, kinder than the cruel ditty sung at Sunday school. When I first heard it, it almost made me smile, but the fact that it was also much harder for folk to get their tongue around gave me more satisfaction!

It is one thing to drive oneself with the desire for knowledge and discovery. It is quite another to have others pushing and demanding and criticising. Only Elizabeth understood how hard it was for me, with all the warring Marys in my head – the one who despaired of ever finding anything of such import ever again; the one who despised the gawpers and hated the pressure to earn money, wasting time which might have been spent learning and studying and being a true scientist; the one who fought back the tears at the loss of Father; the one who wondered what manner of creature she herself was. Sometimes, their clamour drove me near to madness. There was no peace from them, it seemed.

But time passed. Weeks turned into months and, as the attention lessened, I did what had to be done with little or no expectation placed on me by others, beyond the pressure from Mother to make money. I found nothing worth more than a few pennies, but some people still made a point of visiting and we sold enough to keep the wolf from the door. Elizabeth and I must have found a thousand ammonites between us. They always sold well.

Elizabeth was my saviour, for together we passed our days searching and our evenings reading and talking about science and our discoveries. Henry's letters were few and far between and his mother was more often in London than Lyme, so the bonds of that friendship of which he claimed to be so fond seemed to be fraying to nothing. It was to be expected, I supposed. Hadn't Father warned me that people change and loyalties are forgotten or betrayed?

Elizabeth and I worked well together, for her passion was more for fish preserved for ever in their slate graves, like silvery ghosts, so she was happy to yield other finds to me. Her own collection grew apace. The one cabinet in her library on Silver Street became three, then five, and then the whole house was quite taken up with her collection. Visitors ogled and marvelled at her specimens and then she sent them down to my table on the beach and they spent their money on shells and snakestones and the like. Oh, I knew what those things were, the ancient oysters and cuttlefish with their fancy Latin names, but I was resigned to the fact that *Devil's toenails* and *ladies' fingers* and *thunderbolts* made a better story for fancy folk and Mother and I could spin a spine-chilling yarn when it suited.

Sometimes I would find myself questioned by gentlemen who, like Buckland, had a scientific interest in my finds. Elizabeth told me they admired me greatly, but it seemed to me they were like the seagulls, happy to steal a meal that someone else had caught, for they asked their questions and gleaned my knowledge with no genuine regard for my ideas or labours or any thought to reward these in the only way that made any real difference to me – coin. 'Fine words butter no parsnips,' as Mother often said. 'Talk is cheap,' she might have added, for talk was all they offered me, unlike Elizabeth who gained her reward from her pleasure in sharing her knowledge with me.

On fine, dry days, I would get up before the break of dawn and walk along the beach, while all was quiet and still and free from visitors and fancy folk and all the Marys in my head would be at peace, particularly if there had been a storm the night before. A storm throws everything about so, yet when it has passed, there is a stillness like no other, a freshness as if all has been washed clean and laid out anew.

It was not long after my sixteenth birthday that I came across a poor drowned woman, delivered up by the tide, lying in the shallows. She was quite the most beautiful woman I had ever seen. I crouched by her side and gazed on her for many minutes. Her skin glowed white as the moon. The sea had dressed her in sea lettuce and bound her hair with bladderwrack so that she seemed half-sea creature, half-human. I felt a great wave of sadness wash over me that such a beauty, such a treasure, should now be doomed to decay. No slate bed for her. No transformation into rock. No volcano to lift her up and entomb her in the pages of the Earth's history book.

How little time we have.

I gently pulled the seaweed from her hair and closed her blue unseeing eyes and laid her out as best I could.

I paid men to come and place her body in the church, in hope that someone might claim her but no one did. For four days, I took lavender and sweet peas from Mrs Stock's garden to strew around her corpse. I did not know then why I felt compelled to do so and I do not now, but she occupied my thoughts to the exclusion of all else until they laid her in the ground.

Then her true identity was discovered. Her name was Lady Jackson. She was a mother and a wife. She perished with all her children when their ship was lost off Portland. All that way from India, to be drowned a mile from home. Wiped from the Earth as if she had never existed. How utterly without purpose.

I thought of her beautiful face, frozen like marble, wrapped in seaweed. I thought of Henry and his stories of sharks and hungry sailors and of his mother in her black gown and of Mother with that bundle, the scrap that was barely there, and I looked down at the ammonite on its leather necklace, hanging near my heart, and I cried and cried for Father and all that was lost for evermore and then I dried my eyes and went back to work.

'We were worried about you,' Elizabeth said, as we set off towards Monmouth beach one morning, shortly after the funeral.

'Nothing ever came of worrying,' I replied.

'That poor woman and her poor children. You showed her great kindness, Mary, but I worry at what cost?'

'Cost me next to nothing,' I said, not wishing to be drawn on the subject.

Elizabeth knew better than to speak to me of such things but she continued, nonetheless. 'I did not mean money, Mary. There are costs to our person in pain and suffering, as well you know. I wondered if you felt as I did, that our lives could end at any moment? You have already had so much to bear, and now this! Our time here is precious and you are young, Mary. You have your whole life ahead of you.'

'I do indeed, as do you,' I replied, feeling a tightness in my chest as I spoke. 'We all have our lives ahead of us 'til we be

234

dead and, as you say, we could be dead tomorrow, so being young is neither here nor there.'

I started digging with great vigour, hoping she would stop with this talk which made me want to stop up my ears and scream.

'But you *do* have your whole life ahead of you, Mary. Do you consider what might be done with it? What contribution you might make? Do you not consider that?'

'I do not. The days dawn. I fill them with searching or selling. They are either good days or bad days. Nothing I think, say or do will make them any different. Such is my lot. The life before me is the same as the life behind me, save I am older, another step nearer my Maker.'

I hoped this would end her prying, but something of what she said had got into my head like grit in an oyster shell. Was this really my lot? Was this why I had been spared death by the lightning's strike? Was I part of God's plan and if so, why did He torment me so by showing me things which made me question everything and doubt everything?

Sometimes it felt to me as if God were like the sea: cruel, changeable, heartless, creating and destroying; and yet these thoughts could only be the Devil's work, surely?

Faith and science. Science and faith. They seemed at war in the world and in my head.

*

For the next few days I worked alone and I was glad of it, for my mind was in a turmoil. Elizabeth had gone to Oxford to take William Buckland a very fine ammonite specimen (that I had found and cleaned) and to attend a talk he was giving at his college. For all I valued my solitude, I envied her this time spent with people of high intellect, people who knew things and took pleasure in knowledge for its own sake, with no need to turn it into money, people who were, seemingly, untroubled by the torment of doubt. Maybe the company of such people would have taught me to better express myself, for I had ideas aplenty in my head, all the time. As it was, I lacked the skill or the practice to give voice to them out loud and something brusque or cross-sounding usually came out, unless I was speaking with Elizabeth. My letters to Henry, infrequent as they were, could not help me untangle all the thoughts that buzzed about in my head.

I returned to The Spittles, the scene of my so-called triumph four years before, in search not of a monster but some quiet in which to organise my mind. The sky was a mass of deep blue grey clouds above me, heavy with rain; but away over towards Golden Cap the sun shone and the grass was as bright green as a new beech leaf.

Was that my lot? To work under a cloud with the sun and the green fields for ever at a distance, out of reach? To be an object of curiosity? The child-woman who found what . . .

one of God's mistakes? What if that discovery were never to be repeated? What if that Fish Lizard was the only monster to be buried in the cliffs?

All my instincts told me that it was not so. All my studies, my discussions with Elizabeth, told me it was not so and yet to prove it so would take all my strength, all my youth and for what? So others might claim the glory?

There was a break in the cloud and all of a sudden I had that feeling in my bones again, a feeling that there might be something about to happen, something that might bring change. I felt my father's eye upon me and looked around as if to find him there.

Nothing.

Then I heard footsteps in the distance and the quick, shallow panting of a dog. I stood up to see who was coming to disturb my work and my thoughts.

A tallish man, not old, fair-haired and with a spaniel at his side on a leash – a puppy by the looks of it, as it pulled and wandered and wiggled along in an unruly fashion.

I felt irritation rising up inside me. This was my beach. My escape. It was not to be invaded by careless walkers of even more careless dogs.

'Mary! Do you not know your old friend and collaborator?' the figure called out.

The voice was deeper but unmistakably his. Henry!

He reached me, a broad grin spread across his face which was browned by the sun. He made as if to embrace me, but I stepped backwards just in time. I felt myself in danger of being overwhelmed by unwanted feelings of joy, elation, fury and disbelief.

I took a deep breath. 'So. You're back then,' I said, while the puppy sniffed my skirts and wagged its feather tail so hard it was like to knock us all over.

'I am. All too briefly, I am afraid.'

He tried to hold my gaze but I refused to return it and looked out to sea.

'On leave, I suppose.'

'No! Lord, no! Thrown out!' He changed his tone and began to speak in a loud, deep pompous voice such as I have heard many a time amongst the bigwigs. '"*Young man! You are an ill-disciplined fellow and this regiment has no use for you. We can do no more with you. Your career is at an end forthwith!*" Music to my ears, Mary! Music to my ears! So no more falling off Troy for me! No more parades and drills and all that nonsense! Besides, the war with Boney is over and they have no need of me! Bonaparte is defeated and I am free! Like you! And like you, I am going to follow my dream!'

I could not help my bitter laugh. My dream! What did he know of *my* dream? Dreaming is for fools and for those who are asleep, but I bit my tongue and said nothing.

'I have a plan to join the Geological Society of London at the first opportunity!' he continued. 'And I am going to propose that *you* join it too! It is quite new and forward-thinking. We can achieve so much, Mary, and you deserve to be a part of it. You are already famous. Buckland – you have met him, I know – speaks of you often and has the greatest respect for you and I bask in your reflected glory, for I can say that I was not only taught by Mistress Anning herself, but I am also one of her very oldest friends!'

Reflected glory indeed! Henry was as he ever was, a puppy eager to be petted as was the puppy at my feet, squeaking and wriggling and beating its tail fit to burst. Yet, deep down, I was pleased to see him, even though he had such foolish notions of my fame.

I responded part in jest, but part in bitter regret. 'Join your society? Piffle! I am as like to inherit a fortune and be dubbed a lady. And as for glory, it's a fantasy of your own making!'

Henry looked disquieted for a moment. 'But you are consulted, I know! And your ichthyosaur is still quite the talk of London—'

'Only Joseph found it,' I interrupted.

'The skull, yes, but you and I and Buckland know who must take the credit for the entire find.'

'That's as may be, but I have no foolish notions,' I continued, for the unfairness of it all was once again foremost in my mind. 'These bigwig know-it-alls come down from London and Oxford and Cambridge and pick my brains clean as a fish bone all right, but do not deceive yourself that they will admit me to their company for I know they will not. You are older than me, Henry De la Beche, and have more learning than I shall ever have, but for all that you are ignorant of the world and a dreamer of dreams which, for such as I, will never come true. Now, are you going to help or take that puppy home to your mother?'

'Same old plain-speaking Mary!' Henry replied, his face serious and earnest. 'Well, I acknowledge your superior wisdom. It has always been my belief that you are wise beyond your years and mine; but you must trust your old friend to fight your corner, for I will see justice done, mark my words! You are truly a scientist for what you do, not for what people may call you. You must believe that and believe in yourself as I believe in you. And as for this puppy . . . why, he is *yours*. A companion for you!'

He stared at me intently, as if willing me to be as excited as he. I felt vexation starting up in my veins. What use did I have for a dog, especially a fancy, curly-coated spaniel better suited to a hunting man with a servant to keep its feathery legs snowy white? Another mouth to feed. A creature needing my care. The puppy looked at me with its huge brown eyes. It wanted something from me. I had to look away.

240

Henry persisted. 'I like to think he might watch out for you in case of a landslip. He'll guard your life, be your faithful companion in my stead. He is young, yes, but very willing to learn. And he is, as yet, nameless. You can name him, Mary.'

The puppy let out another long squeak and jumped up, its paws against my knees.

'See how he likes you! You must not worry about his keep. Cook is under orders to save scraps so that he may be fed at no expense to you,' Henry said, putting the leash in my hand. 'Keep him by you for my sake, Mary. Please.'

The puppy was sitting now, its soft limbs splayed out, its tail beating the sand.

'He is a little wilful, but that shows character. You can train him, Mary. Remember how you trained me? I became useful to you, didn't I, even though you were not inclined to like me at first!'

I said nothing. I just thought, And what if I should become fond of the creature, what then? For everything I have become fond of is taken from me eventually.

'Well? Will you train him or must I return him in disgrace because he does not please you?'

He stretched out his hand to take back the leash, but I held onto it. Maybe I *could* train the spaniel. As if responding to a command, the puppy suddenly leaped up and started digging in the sand, creating a deep hole in an instant and then sitting back down again in a heap, looking to me as if asking for praise.

Henry laughed. 'You see! He will make a fine apprentice! Now, come, shake my hand, Mary, and trust your old friend to deliver on his promise.'

He was staring at me intently again and once more I had to look away.

I suddenly remembered a question that had burned in my mind so long ago, when Father died. 'You once did a drawing of me and called me Lightning Mary. Why did you call me that? It was only my father ever called me by that name. I suppose you believe that tale, that I was a dull creature before the lightning struck me.'

'Nothing could be further from the truth. I called you . . . *call* you Lightning Mary because you think as fast as lightning, you split rock just as lightning does, and although you had a face like thunder most of the time, you illuminated my life like the brightest of lightning in the darkest days of my life. Lightning Mary seemed then, and still seems now, to be the right name for you. You are a rare creature, Mary. One of a kind. Extraordinary. One day everyone will know it. Of that I am sure.'

He held my hand for a few seconds more, bowed and turned to begin the long walk back to Lyme.

For a while, after he had gone, I lay on my back next to

the exhausted puppy and felt its warmth as it nestled close to me. I spread my fingers out against the sand and stones, as if I were feeling for the beating of the heart of the Earth itself or the breathing of the beasts buried deep in the stone, creatures never before seen by man, creatures so old that my sixteen years were but a day to them.

They were all around me, waiting, waiting to be found, thousands upon thousands upon thousands. Monsters and marvels and mysteries, all waiting deep in the Earth. Waiting for release. Waiting to be marvelled at by men and women and children. Waiting for their mysteries to be revealed and their stories told by the men of science.

And by me.

I thought back to Father's words to me in the workshop. Maybe happiness was not for the likes of us, but maybe there could be contentment in our labours and in the fulfilment of our purpose on this Earth. Why else was I on God's Earth, if not to uncover its wonders? And who else could find these treasures and set them free from their prison of rock but me, Lightning Mary?

AFTERWORD
MARY ANNING: SOME FACTS AND AUTHOR'S COMMENTS

*M*ary was born on 21 May 1799 and at fifteen months survived a lightning strike which killed the woman holding her and two others. Some said it transformed her from a dull child into a bright spark.

Mary grew up in a period of great change in politics, religion and society, much of it against a backdrop of war with the Emperor Napoleon as he attempted to conquer Europe before being defeated in June 1815 at the Battle of Waterloo. Her childhood also coincided with the beginning of the end of slavery. In 1807, the British Parliament passed the Slave Trade Act which banned the transportation and trade in slaves in the British Empire, but slavery itself was only fully abolished in 1833.

The ichthyosaur skull was found in late 1810 or early 1811, just after the death of Richard Anning. Joseph did find the skull and was credited with the entire find when it went on display, but Mary completed its excavation and reassembly in 1811 to 1812. Not much is known about the excavation process except that men were paid to get it down from the cliff, but I think it's entirely feasible that she dared to do much of the work herself . . . though maybe not by abseiling!

Her next big find was in 1823: the complete skeleton of a plesiosaur. This was followed up in 1828 by the 'flying dragon', or pterosaur, and a squaloraja fish in 1829. Over her forty-year 'career', Mary found an absolute myriad of creatures, but these are the most important. None of them, however, bear her name. They were all named after the men who bought them or who announced them – with Mary's permission – to the world. Her gender and low status meant it was unthinkable that she should have anything named after her. Elizabeth Philpot had a fossil fish named after her, but she was 'gentry'. All the men who had dealings with Mary have specimens named after them. Imagine how disheartening that must have been!

Mary did meet Henry De la Beche when she was a child, but I have, of course, imagined their time together (Beche is pronounced 'Beach' – Henry's father added the 'De la' so that it sounded a bit grander!). It is clear that their friendship ran deep and their combination of his knowledge and her instincts was very successful. He always gave her full credit for her contribution and came to her financial rescue more than once, auctioning off drawings of finds and selling off prints to raise money for her.

Henry did not, as far as I know, give her the puppy, but Mary did come to own and train one and called him Tray (a very strange name for a dog!). Tray would sit and guard a find while she got extra equipment or help. Very sadly, he was killed in a landslip which missed Mary by mere feet. It must have broken her heart to see her loyal friend killed doing her service.

Elizabeth Philpot, after whom the Lyme Regis Museum was originally named, was also a good friend and companion to Mary. I have concentrated on her rather than her sisters, Louise and Margaret (who also collected fossils and shells), because there is better evidence through letters etc of her relationship with Mary. The accounts of their conversations are, of course, fiction, as are the meetings with Mr De Luc.

The story of the drowned woman is true. Mary was sixteen years old when this happened. How can it not have had a profound effect on her? It is no wonder that her tender behaviour struck people like Anna Maria Pinney, who became friendly with Mary in her later years, as Mary was generally known for her no-nonsense manner and plain-speaking; not that she was unkind, but she was definitely not one for sentimentality. Anna seems to have thought it was evidence of a romantic streak in Mary's nature. Maybe she felt she was one of the few to see Mary's softer side and felt rather proud of that. But she was also not blind to the way Mary was exploited by some, writing: *'She says the world has used her ill . . . these men of learning have sucked her brains, and made a great deal of publishing works, of which she furnished the contents, while she derived none of the advantages.'*

In 1826, Mary opened her shop, Anning's Fossil Depot, and was sought out by all the leading geologists and palaeontologists. In 1844, King Frederick Augustus of Saxony visited and bought an ichthyosaur skeleton for his extensive collection. The King's aide, Carl Gustav Carus, wrote in his journal: *'We had alighted from the carriage and were proceeding on foot, when we fell in with a shop in which the most remarkable petrifications and fossil remains – the head of an ichthyosaurus, beautiful ammonites, etc – were exhibited in the window. We entered and found the small shop and adjoining chamber completely filled with fossil productions of the coast . . . I found in the shop a large slab of blackish clay, in which a perfect ichthyosaurus of at least six feet was embedded. This specimen would have been a great acquisition for many of the cabinets of natural history on the Continent, and I consider the price demanded, £15 sterling, as very moderate.'*

William Buckland, the first ever Professor of Geology at Oxford University, almost certainly visited to see her first big find, the ichthyosaur, but it did not get its scientific name until some years later. I had Buckland name it then and there for the sake of the story. Mary became great friends with him and his family. His wife, Mary Morland Buckland, was herself a geologist and a scientific illustrator. They were a pretty lively lot and Mary seems to have got a lot out of the friendship, writing to them frequently and, on one occasion, sending them 'a mouthful of kisses'.

I have not introduced another important figure in Mary's story, Lieutenant-Colonel Thomas James Birch, because he did not come into Mary's life until after the episodes at the end of this book. He bailed the Anning family out when a lean year for finds had left them penniless. He sold off a collection of fossils that he had originally bought from Mary and gave the Annings most or all of the proceeds of about £400, which would be equivalent to £11,500 in today's money. He wrote of the family as being the people who *'in truth found almost all of the fine things that have been submitted to scientific investigation.'*

Despite that tribute and the high regard of many other scientists in the emerging field of geology, Mary was never admitted to the Geological Society (in fact, women were only admitted in 1904). However, when she became ill with the breast cancer which would take her life aged forty-seven, members of the Society raised money to help with her living costs. She died on 9 March 1847 and was buried in the graveyard of St Michael the Archangel in Lyme Regis. You can go and see her grave and the stained-glass window installed in her memory in 1850 and partly paid for by the Geological Society. Do visit the museum in Lyme Regis too. It has got a really good section on its world-famous pioneering palaeontologist. Look out for her name against fossils in museums all over the UK, especially the Natural History Museum in London.

Henry De la Beche was loyal to the very end, and in an unprecedented tribute to a non-member (and a woman at that!), read out a eulogy at a meeting of the Society.

It began: *'I cannot close this notice of our losses by death without adverting to that of one, who though not placed among even the easier classes of society, but one who had to earn her daily bread by her labour, yet contributed by her talents and untiring researches in no small degree to our knowledge of the great Enalio-Saurans, and other forms of organic life entombed in the vicinity of Lyme Regis . . .'*

Charles Dickens wrote, some eighteen years later, of another more mercenary reaction to her death in an article entitled: 'Mary Anning – the Fossil Finder': *'Dr. Buckland and Professor Owen and others knew her worth, and valued her accordingly; but she met with little sympathy in her own town, and the highest tribute which that magniloquent guide-book,* The Beauties of Lyme Regis, *can offer her, is to assure us that "her death was, in a pecuniary point, a great loss to the place, as her presence attracted a large number of distinguished visitors". Quick returns are the thing at Lyme. We need not wonder that Miss Anning was chiefly valued as bait for tourists.'*

On the one hand, Mary's story is profoundly sad – or so it seems to me – but on another it is an absolute triumph of one woman's singlemindedness and determination against all the odds. I must confess myself little interested in fossils, but there is something about this lone figure, braving the elements and the treachery of the landscape to uncover the treasures we can now see displayed in museums across the world. Even more gutsy and inspirational is the fact that she did what nobody would have expected from a 'mere' woman and one of a lowly class at that.

She was at the cutting edge of earth sciences at a time when most people took the Biblical description of creation literally. The theories explored in the book John Playfair's *Illustrations of the Huttonian Theory of the Earth* (which I imagined her being given) would have been regarded as incendiary stuff, revealing the Earth to be in a constant cycle of change and millions of years older than the six thousand years most believed the Earth to be. Mary's fossil finds provided evidence for views which challenged these long-held beliefs and sent huge ripples through society and organised religion. The concept of extinction – or, worse, of God making mistakes – was absolutely unthinkable to a Christian and anyone who spoke or wrote about such things was regarded at best as a troublemaker and at worst as a heretic.

It is hard for us to really get our heads round just how extraordinary Mary Anning was as an individual, but when you reflect that, even now, nearly 200 years on, from a numerical perspective men continue to dominate the scientific community, her status becomes even more remarkable. And she was pretty much self-taught – no university for her!

Now that I have come to the end of this book, I find myself missing her feisty, prickly presence. She has taught me the importance of getting on with it, whatever it is ... writing, fossil-hunting ... and of doing something that fires you up and drives you on, through obstacles and setbacks.

Good on you, Lightning Mary!

Portrait of Mary Anning with her dog Tray, painted by B.J. M. Donne

Fossils and Fossil-hunting

*M*ary often refers to the fossils by their local names so here is a brief summary of their formal identities, as well as a few definitions of other geological terms relevant to her:

Angel's wings: Also known as *Fool's Gold*, this is iron pyrite. Not a fossil but a very pretty, shiny mineral.

Its structure is curious, made of very precise geometric forms, including cuboids, framboids (raspberry shapes!) and dodecahedral shapes. I imagine the piece Mary found was particularly large and sculptural. White iron pyrite was popular with the Romans and the Victorians, who made extensive use of it in marcasite jewellery, setting small, faceted pieces in silver.

Coprolites: oddly shaped fossils often found in the region of the abdomens of ichthyosaur skeletons, which Mary determined were fossilised dinosaur faeces. Later named 'coprolites' by Buckland.

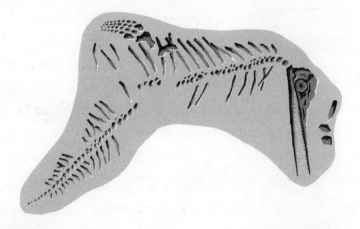

Devil's toenails: the lurid name given to an extinct bivalve mollusc, not unlike an oyster. It looks, at a pinch, like a very thick, greyish-white toenail!

Ichthyosaur: a reptile that lived in the Mesozoic seas while dinosaurs roamed on the land. Extinct for about 90 million years, the specimen found by Mary and Joseph Anning was the first to come to the attention of the scientific community in London.

Mary went on to find further ichthyosaur skeletons.

Scuttles: extinct marine creatures somewhat akin to cuttlefish.

Snakestones and *ram's horns* are both ammonites and the choice of name no doubt referred to their appearance, depending on whether they looked more like a curled-up snake or more heavily ribbed like a ram's horn. Ammonites are the fossilised shells of a group of predators known as *cephalopods*, which includes their living relatives the octopus, squid, cuttlefish and nautilus.

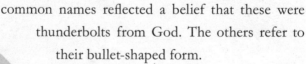

Thunderstones, Devil's fingers, ladies' fingers: belemnites – the fossilised shells of another extinct cephalopod which looked very like a tiny modern-day squid. The first of these common names reflected a belief that these were thunderbolts from God. The others refer to their bullet-shaped form.

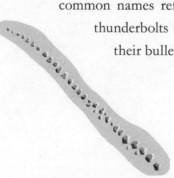

Verteberries (sometimes called *'crocodile teeth'*) were, as Mary learned, individual ichthyosaur vertebrae.

You can go **fossil-hunting** on Charmouth and other Lyme Bay beaches too, but go with a guide. The Blue Lias consists of a sequence of limestone and shale layers, laid down at the end of Triassic and the start of Jurassic times, between 195 and 200 million years ago. It is these layers which make the Jurassic coast such a treasure trove but also means the cliffs are as treacherous today as they ever were. Landslips are not uncommon. People have been killed, and exploring the cliffs on your own is simply not worth the risk.

STEMettes
♥ ★ # +

Stemettes endorses *Lightning Mary* because it tells the story of an inspirational female scientist, Mary Anning, who made numerous discoveries. In the nineteenth century, being female and working class was a tremendous barrier for individuals who wanted to gain an education and develop scientific knowledge. *Lightning Mary* demonstrates that a scientist can come from any background and that age, gender and money should not stop them.

But though 200 years have passed since Mary Anning was a girl, women are still not proportionally represented in Science, Technology, Engineering and Maths fields, collectively known as STEM subjects. Of the people working in the UK's STEM industries, just 21% are women.

Stemettes is a social enterprise working across the UK, Ireland and beyond to inspire and support the next generation of girls and women into STEM industries by showing them the amazing women already in STEM via a series of panel events, hackathons, exhibitions, and mentoring schemes.

If you're a student or school-leaver who would like to find out more about events and schemes near you, check out www.stemettes.org and click on 'Events'.

If you are a teacher, parent or work with young people, please email schools@stemettes.org to find out more about school trips, clubs and visits.

You can also see what Stemettes is getting up to here:
twitter.com/Stemettes
instagram.com/Stemettes

ACKNOWLEDGEMENTS

Ellie Macklow-Smith, daughter of a very dear friend, who read the first few chapters, encouraged me to finish the story and then read the first full draft. Ellie loved Mary's *'sheer feminism'* and that *'she doesn't back down, she doesn't let men and status put her off!'* Mary and Ellie have much in common!

Chloe Sackur, from Andersen, whose editorial notes were invaluable and who saved me from a couple of hilarious continuity errors, including not one but two very temporary babies!

I made use of factual information from the internet and Patricia Pierce's book *Jurassic Mary: Mary Anning and the Primeval Monsters* (The History Press) but for everything else I just channelled Mary and her insistent voice in my head, telling me how it was for her, and of her pain at the loss of her father – something I could identify with only too well.

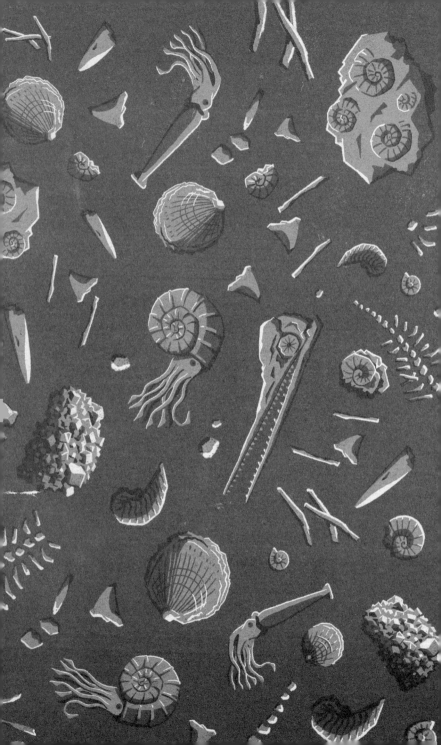

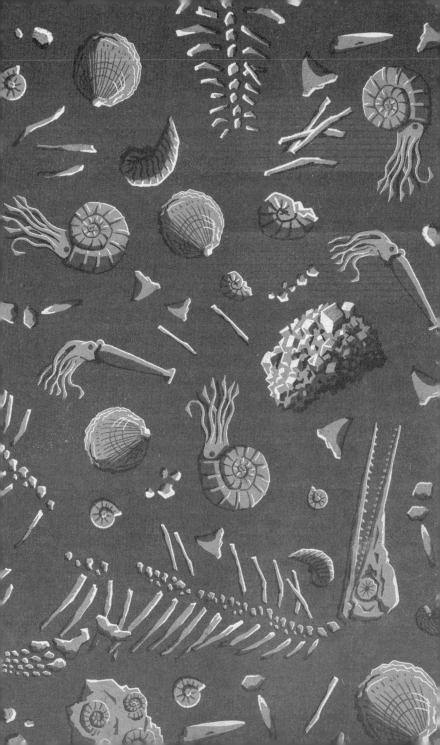

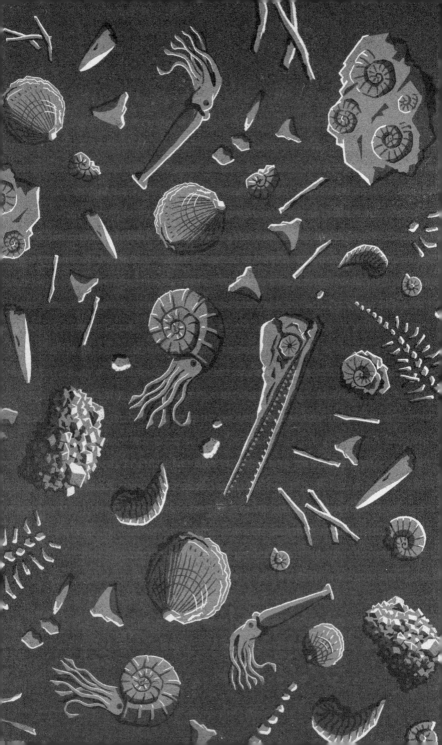